_To_

TEETH OF THE SEA

TIM WAGGONER

Thanks again for the kick-ass blurb! Tim

Tim Waggoner

SEVERED PRESS
HOBART TASMANIA

TEETH OF THE SEA

For Peter Benchley and Steven Spielberg

CHAPTER ONE

The Great Deep

They swam together, the four of them, as they usually did, females in front side by side, males in back. The water was warm and pleasant here, and it spoke to them, welcoming them home.

This island was The Beginning Place, the one from which they had come, and the one to which they must always return. This was the first return for the four of them, though. It had been many years since they had broken free from their shells, dug their way upward through sand, and emerged into the open air. Many years since they had heeded the call of the Great Deep and headed for the water. Creatures of the air swooped down to attack them, hoping to gain an easy meal, only to discover these little ones already had teeth and knew how to use them.

Many little ones were born that day, and once they had swum out far enough, they separated and joined their individual Matriarchs and Sires, and followed them out into the Great Deep.

During their long journey back to The Beginning Place, Whiteback and Nub's two brothers had left their pod in search of egglayers. Before long, One-Eye and Brokejaw had approached, males from a different pod, seeking their own egglayers. Neither was a prime candidate for breeding, but there weren't many of their kind remaining these days, and the females couldn't afford to be choosy. So One-Eye and Brokejaw joined their pod, and they all continued on to The Beginning Place, the males and females mating along the way. Now they were here, or nearly so, their instincts telling them to follow the water until they reached land. Then they would feed to replenish their strength after their long journey, and the females would nest and lay eggs when they were ready.

Large black rocks surrounded the island, rising from the ocean floor and tapering to points in the air. The four maneuvered through the rocks, and once past, they found the water becoming shallower as they neared land. Nub and Whiteback came across the hard thing first – Nub actually bumping her snout into it – and they stopped to examine the strange object. One-Eye and Brokejaw stopped as well, all of them using their flippers to keep themselves in position. They'd followed a strong current here from farther out in the ocean, and they could feel the current continuing on past the hard thing. It didn't make sense. If they couldn't swim past the hard thing, how could the water get through? They needed to swim on, following the current. Their instincts demanded it, and they could no more choose to ignore those instincts than the sun could decide not to rise each morning.

Nub and Whiteback applied themselves to the problem of the barrier while the males looked on. Their species was sexually dimorphic, the females larger and stronger than the males. So One-Eye and Brokejaw kept their distance as Whiteback and Nub backed up and swam full speed toward the barrier. The "hard thing" was a fifty-foot-wide underwater fence made of PVC pipe, and when the sisters smashed into it, they found it wasn't very hard after all. A section of the fence collapsed as easily as if it had been made from twigs, and the females swam on through, the males following. Their instincts told them they had only two things to do now. Keep moving –

– and *feed*.

CHAPTER TWO

Las Dagas, 74 miles off the coast of Nicaragua

"This is as close to paradise as you can get in this world."

Arden glanced sideways at her wife, but she said nothing. Kris sighed with absolute contentment and squeezed Arden's hand tighter.

It wasn't that Arden disagreed with Kris, at least not with her general sentiment. The island *was* beautiful. Palm trees lining the streets. Bright blue sky with only a few scattered white clouds for aesthetic effect. The temperature in the low eighties, humidity a bit high, but the constant ocean breezes – with their mild saltwater tang – kept it from feeling too hot outside. The sun here seemed larger and brighter than at home in Chicago, but Arden didn't know if that was an effect of the island being so close to the equator or simply her imagination.

Arden had never been much of a sun-worshipper. Redheads like her tended to have delicate pale skin which burned way too easily in the sun. Kris, being black, didn't have the same sensitivity to direct sunlight, and she didn't have to slather on nearly an entire bottle of sunscreen on the slim hope that it might prevent her from getting burnt. But that wasn't the main reason Arden didn't share her wife's enthusiasm for the resort. On the surface, Elysium was amazing. Everything – hotels, bars, restaurants, clubs, even the streets and sidewalks – was new, built in the last couple years, and it was so clean she wouldn't have been surprised to learn that late at night crews scoured the island, removing every bit of litter and speck of dirt they found. Most impressive of all were the artificial canals that crisscrossed *Las Dagas*, making it possible for you to travel throughout the entire island by boat if you wished.

But the place was *too* perfect. Elysium – as its website said – had been created to be the ultimate vacation destination for everyone – singles, couples, and families. *Las Dagas* had been uninhabited before construction on the resort began, and because everything had been built from the ground up, it was too planned, too controlled. All surface and no substance. Imperfections and idiosyncrasies were what gave a place character, but as far as she was concerned, Elysium had neither.

But Kris had had her mind set on spending their honeymoon here, and Arden hadn't wanted to disappoint her, so she'd agreed. But now that they were here, Arden was finding it increasingly difficult to plaster a smile on her face and pretend she loved Elysium as much as Kris. But she was determined to do her best. Honeymooning here was Kris' dream, and Arden didn't want to spoil the experience for her. Besides, a happy Kris was more enthusiastic and energetic in bed, and Arden was *definitely* enjoying that aspect of this trip.

It was mid-afternoon, and they were walking down the sidewalk hand in hand, heading for Elysium's Grand Mall – a name which sounded to Arden like a seizure – which lay at the center of the resort to get visitors to spend even more money that they didn't have. Other people were out walking, all dressed in T-shirts, polo shirts, shorts, sundresses, sneakers or sandals. Occasionally, someone went by on a scooter, bicycle, or one of the electric carts people used to get around *Las Dagas* instead of cars. Arden felt a little self-conscious holding Kris' hand in public. Even in Chicago, people would sometimes give them disapproving looks if they demonstrated any kind of physical affection in public, and it was worse whenever they visited a small town. But no one paid any special attention to them here, which Arden appreciated.

At least this place is solidly located in the 21ˢᵗ century, she thought.

They soon came to a canal crossing. The canals on *Las Dagas* measured exactly fifty feet across and ran to a depth of precisely twenty feet – just as they'd been designed. The bridge across the canal rose up in a slight curve – something Arden assumed was supposed to make it seem a bit quaint – and there were gleaming steel guardrails on either side for safety. Steps led down from the street to the canal on both banks, and at the top of the steps, a white metal sign with raised red letters warned passersby that fishing or diving from the bridge was Not Permitted.

Kris tugged Arden toward the stairs.

"Let's go! I want to see the canal close up."

Arden wanted to say, *What for? We've hit the beach every day we've been here, and it's the same water that's in the ocean.* But she smiled and nodded, and Kris led her down the stairs, pulling her by the hand. When they reached the bottom, Arden thought she might find some trash hidden beneath the bridge which the sanitation crews had overlooked, but the grass on the banks was neatly trimmed and as tidy as everywhere else on the island.

They walked to the canal's bank and looked out at the water. It was a rich, deep blue and looked clean, but boats regularly traveled the canal, and Arden wondered what sort of trash people tossed out as they passed. There could be a layer of debris lining the bottom, and no one would ever know. Arden hoped Kris wouldn't suggest going into the water. The last thing they needed to do was wade out into the water and for one of them to step on a broken beer bottle. Then again, as OCD about cleanliness as resort management was, she wouldn't have been surprised if they employed teams of divers to clean out the canals.

There was another red-lettered sign here, this one on a metal post near the bank, proclaiming that swimming in the canals was not allowed. Kris nodded to the sign.

"There's a reason for that," she said. "All kinds of sea life swim through the canals. Even sharks."

Arden gave her a skeptical look. "Bullshit."

Kris laughed. "Just kidding. They have fences installed where the canals open onto the oceans. Nothing larger than a trout can get in."

She reached into her purse, brought out something, and held her hand out palm up to reveal six small stones.

"Where did you get those?" Arden asked.

"I found them near the hotel when I was jogging this morning. If you hadn't been lazy and slept in, you could've got some for yourself."

"I slept in because someone wore me out last night."

Kris gave her a mock frown. "It better have been me."

"Pretty sure it was. Then again, the lights *were* off."

Kris flashed her the middle finger and Arden grinned.

"So … what are those rocks for?" Arden asked.

Kris looked at her as if she'd sprouted a second head. "For skipping. I know you grew up in the city, but you must've skipped rocks when you went to the lake when you were a kid."

"Nope. My mom and dad took me to the beach lots of times when I was growing up, but skipping stones is something I've only seen in movies and TV shows."

"Then it's high time you learned."

Kris selected three of the rocks and handed them to Arden.

"I picked the best ones for you."

Arden wasn't sure what exactly made one rock better than any other when it came to skipping, but she accepted the rocks Kris gave her with a smile.

Kris had been raised in small-town Indiana, where she'd done all kinds of outdoorsy stuff. Of course she knew how to skip stones, and given her competitive streak, she was probably the best in her town at it.

"All right," Arden said, "but you go first and show me how it's done." Part of her felt this was a silly waste of time, but another part of her liked how playful and spontaneous Kris could be, and how she could bring out that side in her – even if she sometimes had to drag it out kicking and screaming.

"Oh, I'll show you how it's done, all right."

Kris put her purse on the ground. She then chose a rock, gripped it between her thumb and first two fingers of her right hand, then transferred the other two rocks to her left hand. She leaned to the side, pulled her arm back, and flicked the rock toward the water. The rock spun as it flew, and when it hit the water's surface, it skipped five times, making it two-thirds of the way to the other side.

"Impressive," Arden said.

She did her best to emulate Kris' technique, but when she threw her rock, it sailed through the air, arced toward the water, and went in with a loud *plunk!*

Arden turned to Kris.

"No comment from you."

Kris put on an innocent expression. "I wouldn't dream of saying anything about how lousy that throw was."

Arden smiled. "Thank you."

"But if I *were* going to say something, it would be –"

Water exploded in front of them as a large shape surged out of the canal toward Kris. Whatever it was, it was *huge*, its elongated mouth filled with teeth.

The creature turned sideways as it came – allowing Arden to see that it had lost an eye somehow. The thing attacked so swiftly that Kris didn't have time to do more than open her mouth – *To scream?* Arden wondered – and then the creature's jaws clamped shut around Kris' torso, and a gout of dark blood shot from her mouth.

Arden couldn't move, couldn't breathe. It was as if a primal instinct that she hadn't known she possessed kicked in, rendering her unable to move. *Whatever you do, don't draw attention to yourself,* it seemed to say. So instead of running to help Kris or simply releasing a scream of horror, Arden stood silent and motionless.

The monster's momentum carried it partway onto the bank, and it slammed onto the ground. The impact caused a number of Kris' bones to break, and a sudden wave of nausea hit Arden, along with a rush of vertigo. Her vision grayed out, and for a moment she thought she might lose consciousness. But her body's survival instinct was too strong. Adrenaline flooded her system, clearing her vision and wiping away the vertigo. It only intensified the nausea, though.

At first, she thought the creature was some kind of crocodile or alligator, but it wasn't shaped right to be either. Its snout was too long, too narrow, and its hide was smoother. But the biggest difference was that the thing possessed flippers instead of legs. The creature was big, maybe twenty feet long, its upper body colored a greenish-gray, its lower a pale white. Green-gray stripes ran along its sides, making it seem like a reptilian version of a tiger. *It's a sea monster,* Arden thought, and although she knew the idea was ridiculous, that such things didn't exist, she could find no other name for the monstrous beast that was killing her wife.

The creature didn't drag Kris into the canal right away. Instead, it laid there, half in and half out of the water, and chewed on her. Arden had thought Kris died instantly when the monster's jaws closed around her midsection, but as the thing ground her wife's body between its teeth, Kris' arms and legs flailed wildly – one leg flopping bonelessly – and she finally managed a scream. It quickly degenerated into a gurgling sound as she coughed up more blood. The sight of her wife writhing in agony as some kind of giant lizard attempted to devour her broke Arden's paralysis. Survival instinct be damned. The woman she loved needed her.

Arden stood only a few feet away from Kris and the monster, and she quickly reached her wife. She grabbed hold of Kris' wrists and pulled, attempting to free her from the creature's jaws. If Arden's mind had been clear, if she hadn't been overwhelmed with panic and terror, she would've recognized how futile this action was. But what else could she do? So she pulled as hard as she could and did her best to ignore Kris' gurgling screams.

As she played her ineffectual game of tug of war with the creature, she found herself looking into its one eye. She had watched a documentary about sharks on the Discovery Channel once, and she remembered how a shark attack survivor had described the predator's eyes as black and empty, without any sign of awareness. *It was like looking into the ultimate nothing,* the man had said. But while this monster's eye was black, it was far from empty. There was no intelligence there, at least none that Arden recognized, but there was an animalistic cunning. She knew the creature was aware of her looking at it, aware that she was attempting to steal its prey. The monster bit down harder, causing more of Kris' blood to splash onto its already gore-slicked snout. This time, Kris' scream came through clearly, a high-pitched shriek of pure agony.

Arden heard other screams then, more distant, and she looked toward the bridge and saw people gathered there, watching the nightmarish scene taking place below them. Several of them had their phones out and were recording the grisly action.

Goddamned social media vultures.

Kris' head fell back and she looked at Arden upside down. Their gazes met and Kris' eyes seemed to plead with Arden to let her go, to stop fighting and save herself. But that only made Arden all the more determined to save her.

The monster's flippers slapped the bank then, and it wriggled its body back and forth as it attempted to return to the water with its prize.

"No!" Arden shouted. Tears came then, streaming from her eyes and running hot down her cheeks. "You can't have her, you fucker!"

She heard another splash and through tear-blurred vision saw a second dark shape coming toward her, its top and bottom jaws misaligned. She thought, *There's more than one.*

And then those deformed jaws closed on her flesh, and all she knew was pain and screaming and blood. She lost her grip on Kris' wrists as she was pulled into the water by the second creature. Her last thoughts were of Kris. Her smile. Her voice. Her kiss. And then darkness rushed in to claim her and she was gone.

CHAPTER THREE

"Keep filming!"

Shayne Ferreira sighed. Unlike a lot of movie actors, he had no interest in being behind the camera instead of in front of it. But Echo wasn't giving him much choice. She might be his girlfriend, but she could be a more tyrannical boss than any director he'd ever worked with.

The two of them stood next to one of Elysium's canals, but there were no streets filled with tourists here. This part of the resort – simply called the West Shore – was the most exclusive area of Elysium, which meant it was also the most expensive. Not that they couldn't afford it. Shayne's last film – a commercially successful but critically panned low-brow comedy called *Genital Hospital* – had added several million more dollars to his already huge bank account. And Echo Amato (real name Irene Anderson) was one of the hottest pop stars on the planet, loved by music critics and fans alike. The amount of money she raked in every year was bigger than many countries' gross national products. Hell, she could probably buy the whole damn island if she wanted.

The West Shore didn't have hotels. Here, there were luxurious houses for rent or, in the case of the very rich, to own. Echo had a seaside mansion that was larger than most of the comedy clubs Shayne had performed in when he'd been starting out. The famous, the wealthy, the powerful – the West Shore was their private playground, and to make sure it stayed private, there was only one access road in or out, gated and staffed by security 24/7. Shayne – who'd grown up on the streets of Philly – wasn't a hundred percent comfortable with the West Shore's vaunted "exclusiveness," but he hadn't shared those feelings with Echo. He didn't want to say anything that might spoil their vacation for her – or which would remind her of his humble beginnings. Echo had started out wealthy, or at least well off. Her family lived in

Bel Air, and she'd attended private schools all the way through college, when she'd dropped out after landing her first recording contract.

Shayne held his phone sideways and tried to keep it focused on Echo, but it wasn't easy. She ran back and forth across the bank, sometimes jumping, sometimes stopping to execute dance moves to music only she could hear. But considering she wore only a very small white bikini, he couldn't complain about the effect her exertions had on certain parts of her anatomy. Echo liked to change her hairstyle frequently, and she currently rocked a head full of bronze ringlets that fell past her shoulders. Her hair looked too perfect, as if it might be a wig, but it was real. It just cost a hell of a lot of money to get it to look like that. She was a beautiful woman and she kept herself in great shape. Shayne carried a few extra pounds and he knew he should make more time to work out with his personal trainer. Whenever he saw pictures of him and Echo together – in tabloids or on celebrity fan websites – he looked like such a chunk standing next to her.

"I'm still not entirely clear on what we're doing," Shayne said.

Echo stopped posing, put her hands on her hips, and gave him an exasperated look.

"I *told* you. We're making a video for my *fans*. I'll post it on my social media accounts when we're finished."

Echo was in her late twenties, but Shayne was in his early forties. He wasn't a Luddite or anything, but he really didn't get the whole "share every mundane detail of your life" aspect of social media. He had a hard time believing that any of Echo's fans – aside from the horny ones who would love to masturbate to a video of her in a bikini with her breasts jiggling – would give a damn about her antics. Right now, she reminded him of a young child acting silly in order to catch an adult's attention. But that was an observation he planned to keep to himself. At the moment, his job was to appease her ego, not challenge it. Although if this kind of shit kept up during the entire vacation, if every moment was just more fodder for *The Echo Amato Show*, he might break up with her once they returned to LA. That would suck, but at least it would get them both some fresh publicity, and what star couldn't use that?

"Okay," he said, "but instead of playing around on land, why don't you get in the water and swim a little?" He gave her a lascivious grin. "You know how good you look when you're wet."

She scowled, but he could tell by the twinkle in her eye that she liked what he said.

"But what about my hair? The saltwater will ruin it."

"So? It'll give you an excuse to get it done again."

She grinned. "All right. Just make sure you don't miss any of it."

Echo had been on the swim team in high school. In fact, she'd been captain (of course). She strode to the water with confident grace and continued walking until it was up to her shins. Then she put her arms out, curved her back, and dove under, making only a minimal disturbance in the water. Shayne – still holding his camera up and recording – walked to the water's edge to get a closer shot. He wasn't an especially strong swimmer, and he hadn't swum the canals himself, but from what he understood, their currents weren't very strong. So, for an experienced swimmer like Echo, swimming in the canal should be as safe as taking a stroll in the park.

Echo broke the surface at the midpoint between shores and began a relaxed freestyle stroke. She moved through the water as if she'd been born to it, and not for the first time Shayne thought she could've been a competitive swimmer if she hadn't chosen to devote her life to music and performing. Who knows? She might've even been Olympic material. As he watched her on the camera's screen, he thought, *Yeah, she can be self-centered sometimes, but overall I'm one lucky sonofabitch to be sleeping with her.*

Echo shot straight up out of the water, and for a split second, Shayne thought she was executing some kind of elaborate acrobatic maneuver, but then he realized that there was something under her, something that had hold of her in its elongated mouth. The creature was ivory-white, top and bottom, and it surged upward far enough for Shayne to see its front flippers. The appendages quivered as if the beast was excited. Shayne didn't feel anything at first. Partly because of the shock at seeing the woman he ... well, maybe not *loved,* but cared for a hell of a lot, in the jaws of some kind of sea monster. And partly because he couldn't bring himself to believe the damn thing was real. He lived in LA and worked in Hollywood, the dream factory of the world. That creature was nothing more than a special effect of some kind, a mechanical monster like the shark in *Jaws.* Echo had probably set this whole thing up as some kind of prank on her fans – and him. Why else had she been so insistent on his recording her today?

You suggested she get in the water, he reminded himself. *It wasn't her idea.*

More details began to register on his consciousness then. Blood streaming from the places where the monster's teeth penetrated Echo's flesh. The way her arms and legs flailed wildly, as if her nervous system was overloaded with pain and was short circuiting. And then, finally, she screamed.

Echo Amato was known for many things: her passionate support of animal rights, her ability to sing in concert without lip synching, no matter how strenuous her choreography, and the five-octave range of her voice. She could hit high notes that seemed impossible for a human throat to produce, but she outdid herself with this scream. It was, Shayne felt certain, the highest note she'd ever hit, so shrill and sharp that hearing it was like having two ice picks shoved into his ears.

He was still recording as the monster reached the apex of its jump and began to descend. But before it could fall all the way back to the water, a *second* beast – this one a gray-green on top and white underneath – leaped out of the water near the ivory-colored one. The two-toned monster opened its jaws wide and tried to snatch Echo away for itself. But the ivory monster turned its head to the side, and the second monster missed, its jaws snapping shut with a loud *clack.*

Echo was still shrieking when the monsters hit the water. Even though the creatures were in the middle of the canal, the impact of their combined bulk was enough to send saltwater spray splashing onto Shayne. The water was warm, but it hit him like a slap and pulled him out of his shock. The beasts were gone, and Echo's voice had been silenced.

He called her name, lowered the phone, and started wading into the water, as if intending to find Echo, grab hold of her, and carry her back to shore. But then he remembered the monsters, how big they were, how many teeth filled their long mouths, and he especially remembered how the second creature hadn't managed to get a piece of Echo. The beast was still out in the canal somewhere, no doubt still hungry. Feeling like the world's biggest coward but unable to stop himself, Shayne spun around and hauled ass back to shore. Once on land, he kept going until he was a dozen yards from the water, and then – heart pounding in his chest like it might explode any second – he turned back around and scanned the water for any sign of Echo and the two monsters. But he saw nothing. Even the waves caused by the creatures hitting the water were gone.

He realized then that he still held his phone. He lifted it up, looked at the display, and saw that it was still recording. He hit STOP, and then, feeling numb and disconnected from reality, as if were inhabiting in a dream, he started walking back toward Echo's house. A few seconds later, he was running.

CHAPTER FOUR

Holloway, Ohio

"And this is where you saw the creature?" Joel asked.

"Yessir," said Ricky White, a mountainous man in his fifties with a long white beard dusted with black. "This is where I saw the Gork. Damn thing nearly killed me."

Joel and Ricky stood on the side of a country road several miles outside town. Owen Rogers was recording them with a video camera while Pam Powell – Joel's producer – stood next to him, looking down at her phone instead of paying attention to what was happening. Parked nearby was the crew's van, *The Hidden World* painted on the side in green letters that were, at least theoretically, supposed to be spooky-looking. They'd followed Ricky out here from town, and his red pickup – a brand-new model instead of the clichéd country junker Joel had expected – was parked in front of the van.

Ricky wore blue-jean overalls, a white T-shirt, and a Cincinnati Reds ball cap. His teeth were yellow and he was missing a couple in front. But he had a Master's degree in economics and taught at a nearby community college. *A study in contrasts, this man*, Joel thought.

"Can you describe the encounter?" Joel asked. He did his best to sound interested. More, to sound *intrigued*, as if he couldn't wait to hear the man's story. But he was afraid he sounded as bored as he felt, no more life to his words than someone placing an order at a drive-thru.

This area was wooded, with large oaks and elms lining the road, but it could hardly be called a forest. Mostly, the land outside town was taken up by farmers' fields or nondescript ranch homes with old rundown cars parked in the yard. Hardly the sort of place a Bigfoot knockoff would live.

At least the location is nice, he thought. And the weather, while a touch chilly, wasn't bad. They'd filmed in worse conditions than this, more times than he liked to remember. And he was used to listening to liars and loons, since almost every person they interviewed fell into one category or another. Sometimes both.

Joel Tucker was the host of *The Hidden World*, an unscripted cable program that investigated reports of cryptid sightings. The show wasn't a ratings blockbuster by any means, but it had a small but loyal following, and thanks to them, it had remained on the air for five seasons. Joel liked to think of himself as having an open mind, but the longer he stayed in this gig, the more difficult it was to take any of it seriously. Pam and Owen had been with him the entire time, and while they'd investigated some intriguing cases, most of them were like this one: a weird story told by an equally weird person without anything remotely resembling physical evidence. They'd done episodes on all the usual suspects: Bigfoot, the Loch Ness Monster, the Yeti, and by this point, they were scraping the bottom of the barrel for new cryptids to feature on the show. Last season, they'd even done an episode on the goddamn jackalope, for Christ's sake. Now here they were, in southwestern Ohio, talking to a hillbilly college professor about a creature called the Gork.

Somebody shoot me now and put me out of my misery, he thought.

"Well, last summer I was over at a friend's house for a poker game. Nothing big, just penny-ante shit. We'd been playin' for a few hours, and I guess it was probably about one or two in the morning. I had a lousy hand, so I folded and stepped outside to have a cigarette. I don't smoke inside. It's not polite, you know? So I was standin' on the back porch, looking up at the night sky. There were no clouds, and the moon was almost full. Lotsa light to see by. There's a small woods out behind my place, and as I was standing there, I saw something come out of the trees and start walkin' toward me."

Despite himself, Joel was being drawn in by Ricky's story, and from the looks on Pam's and Owen's faces, they were, too. This was the best part of the job. The moment when people began to tell their stories and – for a few moments, at least – you could fool yourself into believing they might be real. The anticipation, the suspense, the wonder … in a way it was like being a kid again and listening to a spooky story told around a campfire. But there was more to it than that for Joel. Every time he heard an eyewitness account, he couldn't stop himself from hoping that maybe *this* time it would be real, and he would finally be vindicated – if only in his own eyes.

"It looked like a man for the most part. Same basic shape, but tall and skinny, like a skeleton covered with skin. 'Cept it wasn't *human* skin. It was rough and pebbly, kinda like rhino hide, you know? Its fingers were really long, and they had extra joints in 'em, and the nails were curved and pointed, kinda like bird claws. It didn't have any hair on its body, and its head …"

Ricky paused and let out a shuddering breath, as if he didn't want to remember this part. Joel looked at Pam and saw she was grinning. This was good stuff, and she knew it. Maybe this episode wasn't going to turn out to be the steaming pile of horse shit after all.

"Its head was misshapen, like an upside-down triangle, and its slit of a mouth was filled with tiny sharp teeth, like a piranha's. The worst part was its eyes – they were pinpricks of red light sunk deep in hollow sockets."

Joel felt a chill ripple down his back, and now he grinned as well. This shit *was* good.

Ricky continued. "I'd heard about the Gork all my life. Who 'round these parts hasn't? But I always figured it was just a story older kids told to scare younger ones. But when I saw that thing comin' toward me, I knew that was what I was lookin' at: the goddamn Gork in the flesh. I ain't ashamed to admit I was scared shitless, and I threw my cigarette into the yard and ran around the side of the house. It didn't occur to me to warn the other guys inside about the Gork. I wasn't really thinkin' straight, you know? I just had to get the hell out of there. I headed for my truck, got in, and started 'er up. I pulled out onto the road, hit the gas, and roared off, tires squealin'.

"I drove like a madman, not really headin' anywhere in specific, just wantin' to get as far away from the Gork as I could.

I drove for a bit, and just as I was startin' to calm down and let off the gas a little, I looked at the rearview mirror, and saw a pair of red dots reflected there. It was the Gork! At first, I thought the goddamn thing was chasin' after me, running down the road super-fast, its long legs pumpin' like crazy. But the eyes were too close, and I realized what had happened: the Gork had managed to climb into the bed of my pickup before I pulled onto the road, and it had been ridin' back there ever since."

Pam glanced at Owen as if to make sure he was getting all this, and without taking the camera off Ricky, he gave a slight nod to indicate he was.

"It started tapping its claws on the back window then, like it was tryin' to get my attention, and it made a sound ..." Ricky shuddered at the memory. "I don't know if I can describe it. A cross between a bird screech and a lizard hiss is the best way to put it, I guess. The sound was so loud I thought both my eardrums would burst, and without realizin' I did it, I yanked the steerin' wheel hard and put us into the ditch." He pointed. "Right here."

Joel and Pam turned to look at the spot Ricky had indicated, and Owen swung the camera to get a shot of it. There was nothing about the ditch to show that the pickup had been here. The grass wasn't flattened, and the ground beneath was undisturbed. But it wasn't as if Ricky's encounter with the Gork had happened yesterday. According to him, it had taken place almost a year ago. Still, they couldn't help looking for some sign of physical evidence. This was, after all, what they did for a living.

When Ricky didn't go on with his story, Joel prompted him.

"What happened after that?" he asked.

"Well, I sat there for a few seconds tryin' to gather my wits. I keep a pistol in my glovebox, so I grabbed and got out of the truck. I figured it the Gork was gonna try and make a meal out of me, I was gonna make sure he had to work for it, you know? But when I looked into the cab, I saw it was empty. I looked around, expectin' the Gork to come runnin' at me from some direction, but I didn't see anything. The road was empty, and there was nothing standin' in the ditch on either side of the road. I thought maybe the Gork had gone into the woods, but I wasn't about to go in after it. I got back in the truck, put the gun on the seat beside me, and drove off. I kept lookin' in my rearview mirror all the way home, afraid that I'd see those red eyes again, but I never did. I got home safely, and I stayed up the rest of the night, sitting at my kitchen table with my gun in front of me in case the Gork decided to pay me another visit. But he didn't. I don't think I slept for a week after that, but I never saw the Gork again. I still have trouble sleepin' sometimes, you know?"

No one said anything for several moments. It was Owen who finally broke the silence.

"That was a great fucking story," he said.

Ricky grinned. "Was it? I was afraid you guys wouldn't like it."

Uh-oh. Joel exchanged a worried glance with Pam.

"Why wouldn't we like it?" she said.

"Well, it's not like I'm a writer or anything. I mean, sure, my buddies say I'm pretty good when it comes to tellin' a story, but that's not the same thing as bein' a professional, you know?"

Joel started to get a horrible sinking feeling in his gut.

"Are you saying that you … made up that story?" he asked.

"Well, yeah," Ricky said. He frowned, looking confused. "These kind of shows are just entertainment, aren't they? Everything's staged. That's why you guys always end your program by givin' your web address and asking people to email you if they've had a 'mysterious encounter.'" He chuckled and shook his head at the ridiculousness of it all. "So how much do you guys pay? I like teachin', but you can't get rich at it."

Ricky grinned, and Joel let out a heavy sigh.

* * * * *

Ten minutes later, they were back in the van – which Owen insisted on referring to as the "Cryptid-mobile" – and on the road once more. Joel drove, Pam rode shotgun, and Owen sat in the back, reviewing the footage he'd recorded on the video camera's display.

"How about we stop at the college where Ricky teaches?" Owen said. "I wanna shoot some b-roll there."

Joel didn't take his eyes off the road as he answered.

"Forget it. We got what we needed."

"*Pam* …" Owen said, sounding like a whiny child – which was ironic given that at fifty-two he was the oldest of the team. African-American, thin, clean-shaven, always clad in flannel shirts, jeans, and scuffed cowboy boots, he looked like he should be working on a ranch instead of standing behind a camera. But despite the fact he shot video for a low-rated and even lower-budgeted cable TV show, Owen considered himself a true artist, and he could get pouty if he felt his freedom to create was being stifled.

Pam raised her hand, a gesture she made whenever she wanted one of them to calm down. Owen let out an unhappy grunt, but he let the issue go.

"It's going to be a decent episode," she said, looking at Joel. He could feel her eyes on him, but he continued facing forward. He knew from experience that whenever you met Pam's gaze during an argument, she had pretty much won the battle. She was kind of like Medusa that way.

Pam was twenty-eight – seven years younger than Joel – but she had the world-weary attitude of someone who'd worked in television for decades. *Producing cheap-ass reality shows isn't for the weak,* he thought. Then again, considering that she had to babysit both him *and* Owen, it was a wonder she hadn't quit show biz and gone into a saner profession, like wrestling rabid crocodiles blindfolded. She was short, with curly brown hair and a dusting of freckles on her cheeks. Perpetually cold, no matter the season, she always wore long-sleeved shirts – usually with a sweater and jacket over them – and slacks. In all the time they'd worked together, Joel had never seen her arms and legs uncovered, even in the worst heat. He'd often thought that she would happier producing a show in Antarctica.

"It's going to be a piece of shit," Joel said, "and you know it. We didn't find anything even approaching a *shred* of credible evidence. Just a bunch of stories from people who were probably laughing at us inside the whole time we spoke with them. Or people like Ricky, who think we pay for interviews."

Pam sighed. "Do we really have to have this conversation again? People watch shows like *The Hidden World* –"

"Because they want to imagine that weird shit really exists," Joel finished. "They don't care if it really does."

"More than that, they'd be disappointed if it *was* real," Pam said. "Things like the Gork are fascinating *because* they're a mystery."

"You gotta admit," Owen said, "the Gork *is* kinda lame."

Joel couldn't help but laugh at that.

Neither Pam nor Owen understood why he'd created *The Hidden World* in the first place and what he hoped to accomplish with the program. To them, it was just a job. But it was so much more to him. He wasn't sure why he'd never told them. Maybe he was afraid they'd make fun of him, or worse, lose respect for him. Or maybe he didn't want to say anything because he doubted his own motivations. Now *that* was a depressing thought.

"All right," Joel said. "I guess we can spare a half hour for our beloved video jockey to shoot footage of bored college kids shuffling around campus and staring at their phones like zombies."

"Yes!" Owen said. Joel saw him do a fist pump in the rearview mirror and smiled despite himself.

A text alert dinged.

"Speaking of phones ..." Pam removed hers from her pocket and checked the display. She didn't say anything for several moments, and Joel glanced over at her. She held the phone close to her face, as if she were trying to get a better look at whatever was on the screen. Her eyes were wide and her lips parted, as if she couldn't believe what she was seeing.

"Pull over," she said softly. When Joel didn't respond right away, she raised her voice. *"Pull over!"*

CHAPTER FIVE

Two miles off the Nicaraguan coast

Lara Rivera stood on the bow of the *Wayfarer,* the ship swaying gently with the rhythm of the waves, ocean breeze caressing her nearly naked body, sunlight coating her skin like warm honey. She imagined most people in the world would kill to trade places with her right now – which was ironic, since she'd kill to trade places with *them*. It wasn't that she didn't love the ocean. After all, she'd practically been raised on water, had spent more time on it than she had land. But that was the problem. You could get tired of anything if you spent too much time doing it, including sailing the Pacific. Especially if what you were doing was boring as hell.

Lara was twenty-nine, tall and slender, with long blonde hair and skin as brown as a nut from all the sun she got. Supposedly too much sun exposure aged skin prematurely, but if so, it hadn't caught up with her yet. She looked younger than her years, and it wasn't uncommon for people to mistake her for a teenager. Other women might have found that flattering, but she found it annoying. The white bikini she wore was so small she might as well have been wearing nothing at all. She wasn't self-conscious about her body, but neither did she like to show it off. She'd been on the deck of one ship or another since she was a child. She'd run around in her panties when she'd been a toddler, and she'd never been comfortable wearing too much when she was out on the water and the weather was nice, like today. It wasn't like she had to worry about anyone ogling her on the *Wayfarer,* though. She and her father were the only members of the crew, and as absorbed as Dad was with his work, she figured she could walk around stark naked if she wanted to and he wouldn't notice. She didn't, though. That would be creepy.

For the last hour, she'd been on lookout duty, and of all the tasks there were to do aboard the *Wayfarer*, this was the one she hated most. She'd rather unclog a stopped-up toilet with her bare hands than serve as lookout. Not only was it dull as hell, Dad didn't like her wearing sunglasses while she did it – he didn't want anything interfering with her vision – and the sunlight reflecting off the water always gave her a headache after a while. She could feel the beginnings of a real doozy right now.

Ostensibly, she was supposed to be watching for leatherback sea turtles. The animals were the focus of Dad's current research, and despite the difficulty of observing them in the open ocean, sightings did occur from time to time, and leatherbacks *were* known to swim these waters. She carried her phone tucked underneath one of her bikini bottom strings, so if she did get lucky, she'd be able to snap some pictures. But she knew leatherbacks weren't what Dad really wanted her to watch for. No, he had her out her scanning the waves for a fantasy, or – to put it less charitably – a delusion. Dr. Andrew Rivera was rather like Captain Ahab. He was just as obsessed as Melville's character in his way. The big difference was that her father's white whale didn't exist.

Visual and auditory impressions came to her then, so faint and jumbled that they couldn't properly be called memories. Her mother in a dinghy out on the water, wearing a black one-piece swimsuit. She was smiling and waving – at Lara? Maybe. She wasn't sure. The water beneath the dinghy darkening, as something shadowy, something *large*, surged toward the surface. Water spraying, mouth opening, teeth – God, so many *teeth* – Momma screaming once, a short cry swiftly cut off, a huge slap as something heavy, something *massive*, hit the water, and then, and then …

Nothing. That was where these memories, such as they were, ended.

A shark, she told herself. *It was a fucking shark, that's all.*

Despite the sun's warmth, Lara shivered, and she wished she had something to wrap herself in. A sweater, or better yet, a robe. A big fuzzy one. She felt nauseous, and the headache that had been building for the last hour hit her full force. The pain was so sudden and intense that dizziness overwhelmed her, and she felt herself starting to pitch forward over the railing. She wondered if there was something waiting in the water for her down there, something with teeth. She supposed she'd find out in a few seconds.

But then hands gripped her shoulders, steadying her. The dizziness maintained its hold on her for several more moments, but it passed. The pounding in her head didn't subside, though, and neither did the nausea.

"Are you okay?"

The hands gently turned her around and she found herself looking into a man's face. Shaved head, unruly white beard badly in need of trimming. It took her a second to recognize her father.

She smiled, doing her best not to wince at the jackhammer digging at the inside of her skull.

"I'm fine," she lied.

Her father's eyes narrowed, and she knew he was searching her own eyes, looking for the truth. But, of course, he didn't see it there. It was, she thought, a perfect metaphor for his entire life. He smiled, patted her shoulders awkwardly, and then lowered his hands. He'd never been good with the whole physical contact thing.

He was in his sixties, thick-limbed and barrel-chested, looking more like a former pro athlete than a marine biologist. He wore a short-sleeved Hawaiian shirt, khaki shorts, and white sneakers without socks. It was the way he usually dressed, the outfit so common that Lara had come to think of it as his unofficial uniform.

"You probably just got too much sun," he said.

She nodded, immediately wishing she hadn't when the motion set off fresh waves of pain in her head.

"Sure," she said, the word coming out as little more than a pained whisper.

She expected him to tell her to go lie down for a while, but he didn't. Instead, he grinned, and his eyes blazed with excitement.

"Something's happened," he said. "Something *big*. You have to see it!"

He grabbed hold of her hand, turned, and started pulling her toward the cabin. She stumbled after him, her head throbbing so hard she thought it might explode. She wished it would. It would put an end to the pain at least.

"See what?" she said.

"The video – on the Internet!" He sounded as excited as a kid who'd just learned Christmas is going to be extended to an entire week this year.

"Video of *what?*" she demanded.

He answered without looking back at her.

"Of *them!*"

CHAPTER SIX

"You're shitting me."

Ysmin Strauss sat behind her office desk, looking up at Tomas Palomo, Elysium's chief of security. Tomas was a handsome man in his early forties, trim, muscular, clean-shaven, with a full head of thick black hair which she loved to run her fingers through. When they were both off-duty, of course. When they were on the clock, it was all business between them. Well ... *most* of the time. Tomas wore the same uniform as the other security officers on the island: light blue short-sleeved shirt, dark blue shorts, black running shoes. On the equipment belt around his waist, he carried a flashlight, a walkie-talkie, a pair of handcuffs, pepper spray, a telescoping metal baton, and a taser. No gun. The board of directors of the Lexana Corporation, Elysium's parent company, thought having security officers with firearms patrolling the resort went against their slogan: "Paradise Welcomes You With Open Arms." Arms, not *fire*arms. There were guns on the island, of course, but they were kept in weapons lockers in the security station, and only Tomas had access to them. Too bad. Ysmin would've preferred to see Tomas carry a gun. On him, she thought it would be sexy.

But her primary concern at the moment wasn't how Tomas would look with a pistol on his hip. It was the news he'd just given her.

"See for yourself." He took a phone from his pocket and handed it to her. "A number of guests witnessed the attack, and several of them managed to take video of it. We confiscated as many phones as we could as 'evidence,' but there's no way we got them all."

She wanted to snap at him: *Why the hell not?* But she knew why. Some witnesses likely fled immediately after the attack and were gone by the time Tomas' people arrived. Others might have taken video and simply lied about it. In this day and age, there was no way to suppress information. It always got out, one way or another. But what couldn't be suppressed could sometimes be *managed*. If you were smart and fast, and she was both.

The phone wasn't locked by a security code, and Ysmin called up the most recent video and played it. Halfway through, she turned the sound all the way down so she couldn't hear the women's screams. By the time the video ended, her hand was trembling so badly she thought she might drop the phone. She forced herself to watch it again. Not because she wanted to – Christ, no – but because she knew that whatever she did next, she was going to have to justify her actions to the board, and she wanted to make damn sure this video wasn't fake before proceeding any further. When it was finished for the second time, she handed the phone back to Tomas. She was pleased to see that her hand was steady ... more or less. He took the phone and tucked it back into his pocket.

"What the hell *were* those things?" she asked. She'd never seen anything like them before: lizards with flippers instead of feet.

"Beats the hell out of me," Tomas said. "They aren't sharks or crocodiles. They look like something out of a goddamned nightmare, don't they?"

Tomas was a former U.S. marine, and he'd worked in security since his discharge, first as a bodyguard for the rich and powerful, then as the head of his own very successful company. The Lexana had engaged his firm to provide security for Elysium, and Tomas had come here personally to work as a kind of long-term vacation. As far as she knew, he wasn't afraid of anything, but there was a note of wariness in his voice that surprised her.

"Whatever they are, they're some kind of animal, and animals can be dealt with," she said. "Any minute, the board is going to get wind of what's happened here, and they're going to call and demand to know what we're doing about the situation. They'll want as much ammunition as they can get to try to prevent this from becoming a PR disaster. So what can I tell them?"

It wasn't that Ysmin had no sympathy for the two women who had been killed in such savage fashion, or for their families.

But there was nothing she could do for those women. They were dead and gone – and most likely being digested at this very moment – and she had a job to do. She had worked at international resorts ever since leaving college, and Elysium was her first high-profile management position. She wasn't about to have this opportunity fucked up by some goddamned hungry sea lizards.

"I've got people out on the canals looking for the things. And before you ask, yes, they're armed, but they have instructions to keep their weapons hidden from guests unless they absolutely have to use them."

"Good. No need to cause a panic."

Tomas smiled. "Or further damage the resort's reputation if we don't have to, yes? I've also got crews checking the canal entrances to see where these things got in."

"If you find one of the barriers is down, don't replace it," she said. "Maybe they'll swim back out to sea."

"If we don't fix the barrier, maybe more will swim *in*," he countered.

She scowled but didn't press the matter. He continued.

"We've closed the beaches for the rest of the day, and we've closed the canals to all traffic except security boats."

"Good. When you find those goddamned things, kill them on sight. I don't give a damn if they're some kind of rare species. All I care about is keeping our guests safe."

"And your job, too," Thomas said with a wry smile.

She returned the smile. "Of course."

* * * * *

She told Tomas to keep her regularly updated as the day went on. He assured he would, and then left. Normally, she would've enjoyed watching his firm ass as he walked away – his uniform shorts were tight and displayed it well – but she had other matters on her mind right then. If the board didn't contact her soon, she'd have to contact them. But before she spoke with them, she needed to figure out how to play this. Any situation, no matter how awful, could be used to one's advantage. All you had to do was work out the angles.

Ysmin's office was much smaller than might be expected of someone in her position. Her title was "Executive Manager," which meant she was in charge of everything in Elysium. No matter was too large or too small for her attention, and she reported directly to Lexana's board of directors. Because of her status, she should've had the largest, most impressive office on the island, with tasteful – and expensive – décor. Such an office had been planned during the resort's construction, but when she was hired, she told the architects to scrap it and build her something more utilitarian. All she needed to do her job was a cell phone, a computer, and a strong Wi-Fi connection. Anything more just got in the way.

So her office had been built in the Crescent Hotel on the North Shore, in the center of the resort's prime tourist area. There was barely room within for a desk, two chairs – one for her, one for a visitor – a filing cabinet and a small bookcase, both of which were mostly empty. No window. She found that outside views, pleasant as they were, only created distractions. The office's sole decoration was a framed copy of the original artist's rendering for Elysium, and the sole personal touch was a framed photo on her desk of her mother Sofia, who was currently spending several weeks with her third husband in Madrid.

Ysmin knew she was beautiful, but only because people had been telling her that all her life. She was in her late thirties, was bi-racial – her mother was Nigerian, her father German – and she had gorgeous café au lait skin and striking green eyes. She wore her black hair short and used only the most minimal makeup, so little that most people weren't aware she wore any at all. Her only jewelry was small earrings. No rings, no bracelets. Accessories were annoyances. She wore tasteful business suits, usually opting for slacks instead of skirts. The one fashion indulgence she allowed herself was shoes, the less practical and more expensive, the better. Today, she wore a pair of Christian Louboutin patent red sole pumps that had set her back nearly $700, but as far as she was concerned, they were worth every penny. And if she wanted to keep feeding her shoe habit, she was going to have to find a way to handle this crisis and preserve her job.

The board wouldn't care about the dead women. Their first concern would be making sure the corporation wasn't held liable for the deaths due to lax safety procedures, but she wasn't worried about that. She was confident they'd done everything possible to make the island safe for guests. The board's second concern would be to minimize the impact this negative publicity would have on business. That was a trickier proposition. Not many people would be keen on booking a romantic getaway or family vacation in a place where sea lizards chomped on anyone who got too close to the water.

She wondered if the board would be able to convince the public that the attacks had been carried out by more common animals: sharks or saltwater crocodiles. Were there crocodiles in this part of the world? She wasn't sure. She didn't consider the possibility that they could play the attacks off as a hoax. There was too much video evidence, some of which had surely been uploaded to the Internet already. And, of course, the dead women's families would need to be notified, and their horrible deaths at the idyllic ocean resort of Elysium would be big news. She could see the headlines now: *Paradise Welcomes You with Open Jaws.*

But until the creatures – whatever they were – were caught and killed, she supposed they could say they weren't one hundred percent certain what had attacked the women. It *could've* been sharks or crocodiles. It's not as if any of the videos would be professional quality. The one Tomas had shown her had been the best he'd found, and it had been shaky and blurry for the most part. Others were sure to be worse. So they could probably get away with the shark/crocodile story, at least for a little while.

Las Dagas was well away from the mainland, separated from the rest of the world. That was one of its selling points. But no matter how hard anyone worked to make the island safe, there were still hazards. People could drown in the ocean – or the canals – if they weren't careful, and there was always a possibility of a shark attack, rare as they were, or a hurricane. Maybe she could convince the board that these sea lizard attacks fell into the same category. Tragic, yes, but an isolated incident. A freak accident.

And if the creatures turned out to be something *truly* different – and she suspected they might – the board could turn that into a positive. An important scientific discovery would take place on *their* island, making Elysium a household name. They could rebrand slightly, promoting Elysium as not just a relaxation destination but also a place of mystery and adventure.

She nodded to herself. She could make this work ... provided there weren't any more attacks. If those damn lizards started eating guests left and right, no amount of spin would be able to counter the negative publicity. She was just going to have to hope that Tomas and his people would catch those toothy fuckers – and fast.

Her phone vibrated then, and when she looked at the display, she was not surprised to see it was one of the board members calling. Time to make with the bullshit. She took a deep breath and answered.

CHAPTER SEVEN

Shayne leaned against a counter in the large – and mostly unused – kitchen of Echo's beach house, a half-empty bottle of whiskey in his hand, his phone in the other. Echo hadn't been big on cooking and he was a disaster in the kitchen, so they'd either gone out to restaurants on the island or had meals delivered. She could've afforded to hire a cook – hell, a hundred cooks – but she'd fired the last one because the woman had been secretly taking photos of her, some quite candid, and selling them to celebrity gossip websites. After that, Echo refused to hire anyone else to work in her house.

After Echo was … gone, Shayne had run back to the beach house. At least, that's what he thought he'd done. He didn't have any real memory of it. It was like one moment he was staring at the water where Echo had vanished, and the next he was standing in the kitchen, chugging whiskey. He felt cold as hell and his entire body shook. Was he in shock? Probably. He took another swig of whiskey. He wished he hadn't quit drugs last year. A cocktail of a half dozen different pills would go a long way to numbing him a lot faster and more efficiently than booze ever could. Echo had kicked the same time he did, but he'd suspected she might've relapsed. If so, she might have a stash hidden somewhere in the house. He'd look for it later.

He still couldn't believe she was dead, and that she had been killed by some kind of fucking monster – *and* that he was holding the video of her death in his hand. He wanted to smash the phone on the granite countertop, throw it to the floor and stomp on it until it was nothing but shattered plastic and broken electronic bits. But he didn't. He could almost hear Echo's voice.

Don't you dare *break that phone! That video is going to make me immortal, like Marilyn Monroe, Jim Morrison, Kurt Cobain … I'll be a legend!*

The idea was morbid as hell, but he knew it was what Echo would've wanted. Sharing the video of her death with the world would be the ultimate social media statement: *I died as I lived – online.*

He knew he had to do something, but he had no idea what. If something like this had happened back home in L.A., he'd have called 911. Did they even have 911 on the island? He didn't know. They surely had some kind of security, but he had no idea how to contact them. Maybe they had an office where he could make a report, like people did in the movies. Despite his issues with drugs and alcohol over the years, he'd managed to avoid being arrested. Not because cops hadn't caught him driving under the influence of one drug or another, so zonked out of his mind that he could barely talk, but because celebrities are treated far differently than normal people. They could fucking get away with murder – sometimes literally. So Shayne had never seen the inside of a police station. Not a real one, anyway. He'd worked on a couple sets designed to *look* like police stations, but that was the extent of his experience with the law.

I should call her parents, he thought. He didn't know them well, but they were good people and loved their daughter like crazy. He wished he had a relationship like that with his folks. His mom had died in a car accident when he was a teenager, and he hadn't spoken to his father since graduating high school. He wasn't even sure if the old bastard was still alive. He took another swig of whiskey, put the bottle on the counter, and raised the phone so he could call the Andersons. But his index finger hovered over the phone display without touching it. What the fuck could he say to them? *Sorry to tell you this, Mr. and Mrs. Anderson, but your daughter was eaten by a sea monster a few minutes ago. But don't worry – her hair was perfect.*

No fucking way.

So he did what any Hollywood actor would do in a time of great loss and despair: he called his agent. She answered after the second ring.

"Hey, Shayne! I was just getting ready to call you!"

Despite the situation, he smiled. Rita Stokes was one of the best agents in town, but she was so full of shit it leaked from her pores.

"Sure you were," he said.

She laughed. "Actually, this time it's true. A script landed on my desk not five minutes ago. Guess what it's for?"

"I don't care. There's something I have –"

Rita continued as if he hadn't spoken. "*Genital Hospital 2*! They also got a new marketing slogan. 'Turn your head and laugh!' Not bad, eh?"

He groaned. He didn't have time for this bullshit. And yet … there was something reassuring about Rita's words. They were so *normal*. They had nothing to do with Echo's high-pitched screams as sharp teeth pierced her flesh, nothing to do with monsters that burst forth from the water only to sink beneath it again, dragging their prey down with them. He didn't want to disturb that normality, didn't want to break the illusion that everything was okay, that the world was the same as always and not a place where you could be killed in an instant by some kind of fucking monster. So instead of telling Rita about Echo, he decided to play along. Pretending was what he did for a living, after all.

"We talked about this, Rita. I don't want to do <u>any more</u> dumbass comedies."

Her tone remained upbeat as she answered, but Shayne could detect an edge to her words.

"You haven't heard how much the studio is offering."

"I don't care. I just want to do something different for a change. Something that will stretch me as an actor."

Part of him was horrified by this conversation. Echo was *dead*, and here he was talking business with his agent. What did this say about the kind of person he was? How could he be so callous and self-centered? But he was still in shock, still not ready to deal with what had happened. At least, that's what he told himself. Because if in truth he was concerned about his career right now, less than ten minutes after watching his girlfriend die, then he was a way bigger bastard than he'd thought.

"I say this with love, Shayne, but you're a *comedian*, not an actor. Your thing is making people laugh, not delivering dramatic monologues."

Translation: *You can't act for shit.*

Shayne wanted to argue with her, but he knew he didn't have the chops to be a serious actor, not the kind who was a critical as well as a financial success and who won truckloads of awards every year. But there had to be something better for him out there than *Genital Hospital 2.*

"How about action movies? I've always loved them." He had a vast collection of films in the genre, from classics to cheap pieces of crap that were barely watchable. The quality didn't matter. If it was action, he watched it.

Rita laughed. "It's a bit late to rebrand yourself as an action hero, don't you think? Tell you what: I'll keep my eye out for an action-comedy script. How does that sound? In the meantime, I'll send the script for the *Genital Hospital* sequel over to your place. Read it ASAP, and then we'll talk, okay? Love ya, Shayne! You're the *best!*"

She disconnected before he could say anything more.

He stood there, phone to his ear, listening to silence. He felt nothing – no sorrow over Echo's death, no anger at Rita for wanting him to keep making brain-dead comedies. It was as if his mind had overheated and shut down his emotions temporarily to keep his head from exploding. But his subconscious must've remained operational, because an idea popped into his head and just like that, he knew what he had to do.

If he wanted the public to see him as something other than a crude clown, then he had to *become* something different. He couldn't keep Echo's death secret for long. The news would break, and when it did, it would break *big*. And since he'd been present when Echo died – had fucking *filmed* her death, for Christ's sake – the media spotlight would shine on him with the intensity of a thousand suns. When that happened, he could show them the same old Shayne Ferreira, king of gross-out comedy. Or he could show them someone new and different: a man who'd decided to avenge his lover's death by hunting down and killing the monsters who'd taken her life. He'd be a real-life action hero then. Talk about rebranding!

He had no idea precisely *how* he would go about slaying these water dragons, and he supposed there was an excellent chance he *could* get killed in the process. But so what? Live or die, either way he'd become a legend: the Hollywood actor who battled monsters. His fame would increase a hundredfold, and fame was the name of the game, baby.

The first step would be to find out who was in charge of this place, and the second would be to convince them to let him join the efforts to deal with these creatures. He didn't think he'd have too much trouble. He was rich and famous, and more important than that, he was a *star*. He was used to people giving him what he wanted. And if the resort's management didn't want to cooperate with him … well, there was always a way to change people's minds. He thought of the video on Echo's phone, and he smiled.

Echo spoke in his mind then, a purr of satisfaction in her voice.

That's my boy.

CHAPTER EIGHT

Spencer Pittman, wearing only a black Speedo, sat cross-legged on the deck of his X-4 yacht, eyes closed, arms relaxed at his sides. The day was perfect: warm sun, mild breeze, calm water. It should've been absolute and utter bliss, but try as he might, he could not ... fucking ... *relax*. A line of sweat trickled down his spine, and the air carried a stagnant tang, as if there were rotting fish nearby. A lot of them. And to top it all off, he thought he was getting a tension headache. Fan-fucking-tastic.

Spencer had dropped anchor less than a mile off the island's West Shore. He was renting a condo there, and he'd set out from the private docks not long after sunrise. He'd been here since then, swimming, fishing, and sometimes – like now – doing fuck-all. He worked as a stockbroker in New York City, and his job, while extremely lucrative, was also stressful as hell. He routinely worked twelve-hour days, often longer, and when he hit forty-five several years ago, his doctor had told him if he kept up the way he was going, he'd have a coronary before he was fifty. Spencer didn't quit his job. No way was he going to give up the money, and he loved the excitement of it. It was like gambling with other people's wealth. But he'd decided to start taking regular vacations. So he bought a yacht and took all of September off to go sailing, relax, and shed the accumulated stress of the previous year. He had sailed down the coast from New York to Florida, and bummed around for several weeks before sailing home. The trip worked wonders for him, and he'd made it a yearly ritual.

Every year, he chose a different location for his annual getaway, and this year, he'd chosen *Las Dagas*. What a fucking mistake *that* had been. He should've known that an island whose Spanish name meant The Daggers was not going to turn out to be a barrel of laughs. First, there'd been the expense. He'd had to pay someone to sail his boat to Nicaragua and then have it transported across the country to the western coast. Then he'd flown down there and sailed the boat the rest of the way to *Las Dagas*. Elysium's website promised a vacation in the "very heart of paradise," with a "serene atmosphere" and the "deep tranquility of a younger, simpler world." It had sounded exactly like what he was looking for. The resort had been open a few years, though, which should've served as a warning. The place was too new, which meant they probably hadn't worked out all the kinks yet. And then there was that name – *Las Dagas* – inspired by the outcroppings of large jagged rocks that surrounded most of the island. That didn't sound particularly inviting, but he'd ignored the name and came anyway. He'd been here six days so far, and he still hadn't managed to relax.

Normally, there wasn't much water traffic on this side of the island. Sailboats and yachts like his, passengers fishing, swimming, diving, partying, or all of the above. But those rich enough to afford to stay on the West Shore sought privacy as much as pleasure, maybe more so, and they made sure to give each other plenty of space. Over the last hour, though, the tranquility Spencer so desperately wanted had been disturbed by powerboats with ELYSIUM SECURITY painted on the side. The boats crisscrossed the waters offshore, as if searching for something, and all the noise and activity had made it impossible for him to even begin to relax. He tried to ignore the security craft, tried not to speculate as to their purpose – had there been a boating accident of some sort? Were they searching for people lost in the water? – but he failed miserably. The security boats had eventually moved off to patrol another section of the island, and things had been quiet since, but no matter how hard he tried, he couldn't find the inner calm he'd come here for.

But the security craft were only an excuse, and he knew it. This last year had been an especially stressful one for him. His ex-wife had gotten remarried – to his college roommate of all people – and both of his children were in college now. Very *expensive* colleges. And neither of them were exactly dean's list material. To top it off, the woman he'd been dating for the last two years was beginning to pressure him to take their "relationship" to "the next level." Meaning she wanted an engagement ring on her finger, the sooner the better. After going through an exceptionally acrimonious divorce from his first wife, he'd vowed never to marry again. Hell, he didn't even want to share living quarters with a woman. Either he was going to have to give in and start ring shopping, or it would be time to start looking for a new girlfriend. And the older he got, the less enthusiasm he had for the dating scene.

When he was a young man, he'd thought having plenty of money was the key to a happy life. What a fucking moron he'd been.

Something large struck the X-4's port side then, knocking him out of his sitting position. His left shoulder slammed into the deck as he fell, and he grimaced in pain.

What the *hell?* Did some drunk asshole just ram him?

He started to get to his feet, when whatever it was hit the boat again. This time when he fell, his chin smacked onto the deck, knocking his teeth together painfully and causing him to bite a chunk out of his right cheek.

"Fuck!" He spat the word, along with a generous amount of blood and a small bit of flesh.

The yacht was swaying from the double impacts, and the blow to his chin had rattled his head, making him dizzy. These two factors combined to make standing a challenge, but he managed it. The inside of his mouth hurt like a motherfucker, and he suspected he'd cracked a few teeth. His shoulder throbbed, too, and he wondered if he'd broken something there. But none of that mattered right now. He had to find out how much damage his boat had sustained and see if whoever had hit him was hurt and needed help. Although as pissed as he was right then, he wasn't feeling especially charitable toward the fucker who'd rammed him. Still, the code of the sea and all that.

He walked to the port railing, not as steady as his feet as he would've liked, and when he reached it, he grabbed hold to steady himself. His head was throbbing now, and he figured he must've hit his chin harder than he'd thought, maybe even hard enough to give himself a concussion. But as alarming as the thought was, it vanished when he saw the water on the port side of the X-4 was clear. No boat. No wreckage. No people treading water, holding out their hands toward him for help.

Nothing.

He frowned. *Something* had hit his boat. Twice. What was it, a fucking submarine?

Whatever it was struck again, this time on the starboard side. It hit harder than before – *much* harder – and he heard the boat's hull crack like a giant egg. The impact knocked him forward, and while he tried to maintain his grip on the railing, his fingers slipped off the smooth metal and he tumbled over the side. He hit the water with a smack and gasped in surprise, inhaling saltwater. Panic flooded his system, and he coughed as he flailed his arms and legs in a spastic attempt at swimming. He was a good swimmer normally, but this situation was anything *but* normal, and it took him a couple moments to calm himself and get control of his body again.

He needed to get back aboard and radio for help. Something had hit the X-4 hard enough to damage it, maybe even breach the hull. He needed someone to tow his boat back to shore before it sank. And if that wasn't possible, he wanted someone to get his ass off the damned thing before it slipped beneath the waves for good. No going down with the ship crap for *this* captain! The security boats had been all the <u>over</u> the place not long ago and hopefully would still be close by. They should be able to get to him before the X-4 went down – provided he hauled ass. The boat had a bathing platform with a ladder at the stern, and he swam for it now, wincing at the pain in his shoulder and the throbbing in his head. He half-expected there would be another impact to the X-4 before he could reach the bathing platform. He imagined the hull slamming against his head and knocking him out, imagined sinking beneath the water and drowning, without ever knowing what had happened. But no such blow came, and he reached the ladder without difficulty.

As he took hold of a rung and started to pull himself up, he saw that the boat was listing to starboard, and he knew the craft was taking on water fast. He had to get to the radio before –

Some deeply buried primal instinct rose within him and shrieked a warning. He stopped climbing and looked over his shoulder, and what he saw was too much for his conscious mind to process all at once. Something was coming at him – something *huge* – gliding through the water with silent, graceful speed. He thought it was a whale at first, but when he saw its mouthful of sharp teeth, he amended his identification to shark. A big-ass shark. *Jaws* on fucking steroids. Except that didn't seem right, either. The thing's head was long, narrow, and tapered at the snout, more like a crocodile than a marine animal. Then the creature lunged forward, fastened those teeth around Spencer's legs, and pulled him beneath the water.

The pain of those teeth piercing his flesh and muscle was unlike anything he had ever experienced before, and he tried to scream. But as he attempted to draw in breath to voice his shock and terror, he succeeded only in pulling more saltwater into his lungs, and his scream came out as a burst of bubbles. The water surrounding *Las Dagas* was clear as glass, and Spencer could see the blood trailing from his wounds. The blood looked almost black, and it made such interesting shapes as it began to diffuse into the water. His body was pressed back against the right side of the creature's head, and he could feel the slick firmness of its scaled hide beneath him. Its eye was the size of a plate, dark brown bisected by a triangle of black. He looked into that eye, expecting to see a malevolent primitive intelligence gazing back at him, but the eye wasn't focused on him. It was focused forward, at something ahead of them.

Spencer had seen a documentary about survivors of shark attacks once, and he remembered one of the people – a surfer with a huge bite-mark-shaped scar on the side of her abdomen – saying that she'd kept punching the shark that had attacked her in the eye until it finally let her go. He didn't know if the same tactic would work against this creature, but it wasn't as if he had a lot of options. He balled his hand into a fist and swung it toward the thing's eye.

It was difficult enough to build up momentum to punch underwater, and the creature was moving so fast that the current made it even harder. But Spencer gave it his best shot, and managed to land a strike in the corner of the creature's eye, where a tear duct would've been if the thing had been human. The creature blinked and Spencer felt a tremor pass through its body. And then, miraculously, the jaws opened and he was free.

It worked!

He floated forward, blood still streaming from his wounded legs. Part of him knew that there was an excellent chance that he would bleed to death before any help could reach him, but right then, he didn't care. All he wanted to do was get the fuck away from this monster before it changed its mind and decided to start chowing down on him again. He turned and began swimming for the surface –

– and that's when he saw the Matriarch. She was nearly twice the size of the creature that had attacked him, and she floated in the water, her fins waving slowly to keep her in position. Her hide was a mottled white and dark gray, and she looked to Spencer like a cross between a sea turtle and a crocodile, only without the shell. He had no idea what she was, and he didn't care. She was less than a dozen yards away from him, and her brown eyes were focused on him with the precision and intensity of a pair of lasers. He understood then what had happened. The other creature – the smaller one – hadn't let him go because he'd poked it in the eye. It had let him go because it had intended to bring him to the big one all along, like some kind of offering. Or maybe just a snack.

As the Matriarch opened her jaws wide and darted forward, Spencer's last thought was *I'm too rich to die like this*. Except, of course, he wasn't.

* * * * *

The Matriarch swallowed the man in a single gulp, and then the Sire approached her and swam up and down, rubbing his body against hers to show his affection and devotion – or whatever the equivalent emotions were for their kind. She tolerated this familiarity from the male solely because she wished him to continue bringing her food, as was her due. But when he wouldn't stop rubbing against her – when, in fact, he started to get a bit amorous – she slammed her head against his as he passed. While her egg-laying years were not fully behind her yet, the prime of them were. Besides, they hadn't come here to mate with each other. They'd come to see that their progeny successfully laid their eggs here at the Beginning Place, as their kind had done since before the first small mammalian ancestors of the man she had just eaten had been born.

The Sire got the message and moved off, but not too far. His place was at the Matriarch's side – as long as she allowed it, that is.

Together, they swam off in search of more food. The journey here had been long, and like the Nestlings, they hungered. But unlike the Nestlings, they were too large to enter the island's canals to hunt. That was all right, though. There should be enough food offshore. They just had to look for it.

As they moved off, Spencer's yacht sank beneath the waves and slowly descended toward the ocean floor. Neither of them noticed, and if they had, they wouldn't have cared.

CHAPTER NINE

Tomas stood in the runabout as Kristin Taylor, one of his security personnel, piloted the craft. They were moving at a slow speed – little more than a crawl, really – and Tomas had no worries about keeping his footing. Besides, not only was he a former marine, he'd grown up on the Gulf Coast. The ocean was a second home to him.

They were cruising the canals on the southeastern side of the island, searching for any sign of the things that had killed the two women in the video. They were also keeping an eye out for any remains that might turn up. Not only would Ysmin want them recovered so they could be returned to the victims' families, she wanted to make sure no one shot any video of body parts and uploaded the grisly images to the Web. *We've got enough shit to deal with as it is,* she'd said.

Elysium might've been a resort, but in addition to the guests, there were employees who worked in the hotels, restaurants, and shops. This meant that at any given time, there were close to 3,000 people on the island, and Tomas had only one hundred security officers to help him deal with whatever trouble might arise, and of course, not all of them were on duty at the same time. But Elysium was hardly a high-crime area. Even the cheapest resort package was expensive, so the people who came here came to have fun, not to commit crimes, and the resort employees were carefully screened before being hired. Because of this, Tomas and his people mostly dealt with guests who'd had too much to drink or who were reckless – or simply unlucky – and became injured. There was *some* crime, naturally. There always was, no matter where you went, but on Elysium, it was mostly minor stuff: pickpocketing, petty theft, drug dealing … all easy enough to handle. But right now, Tomas had every man and woman he supervised out searching for the creatures, and he'd authorized the use of weapons. Unfortunately, there weren't enough guns to arm every officer. Lexana's board of directors was very conscious of Elysium's image, and they were extremely careful about how many guns they allowed onto the island – even for their own security personnel. Privately, Tomas thought this was ridiculous, but he hadn't lodged a formal complaint. What good would it have done? Because of the board's short-sightedness, only half of Tomas' people carried weapons, so he'd ordered them to pair up: one armed officer with one unarmed. The choices were limited: either a Beretta semi-automatic pistol or a bolt-action rifle. He'd chosen a Beretta, and it rode in a holster on his hip. A rifle might have been a more effective weapon against one of the creatures – especially when firing from a distance – but with his training and background, a pistol was all he needed.

"What exactly are we looking for, sir?" Taylor asked.

"Anything that looks like it wants to jump out of the water and eat you," he said.

Taylor laughed, but Tomas hadn't meant it as a joke.

As they patrolled, he was aware of the guests watching as they passed, standing on bridges or lined up on streets next to the canals. How much had they heard? Did they know two guests had disappeared and were presumed dead? Had they seen the fucking video? He looked at their faces, but he saw no signs of fear there. Good. He didn't need to deal with an island full of panicking guests right now. One thing that bothered him, though – bothered him a *lot* – was the lack of any barrier between the canals and the streets. When he'd first taken this job, he'd asked Ysmin why there was no fencing to prevent guests from getting to the canals, especially since swimming wasn't permitted in them. *The whole point of the canals is they're beautiful to look at. Fences would just get in the way of the view.* He wondered if the board – or more likely, the board's lawyers – were mentally kicking themselves for not installing fences when they'd had the chance.

They moved through the canal slowly, Tomas scanning the water for any sign of the creatures and doing his best to focus on the task at hand.

After working in silence for a while, Taylor spoke. "Are you all right?"

It took a moment for hers to register.

"Of course," Tomas said. "Why do you ask?"

"I don't know. There was something about the expression on your face …" She shrugged, as if she couldn't find the words to fully express what she meant.

Tomas gave her what he hoped was a reassuring smile. "I'm fine." He then returned to scanning the water. But he wasn't fine, was he? In fact, he was the furthest thing from it.

* * * * *

Tomas had grown up on Miami's beaches, had spent as much time in and on the water as he had on land. His mami had joked that he was born half fish, but whenever she did so, his abuela had chided her.

"Don't say such things! They might hear your words and think Thomas is one of them. They might decide he should join them beneath the waves, and one day when he's swimming, they might drag him down into the darkness where they live."

Mami would get angry with Abuela for scaring him with her "old woman's superstitions," and while her words *did* scare him, they did so in a delicious shivery way that made him want to hear more. So one day, when Mami was at work and he was home with Abuela, he asked her who *they* were.

She'd looked at him, eyes narrowed, as if she were studying his face. He was thirteen that year, and she said, "I suppose you are near enough a man for me to tell you. You know I lived in Puerto Rico when I was a girl, yes? My papi was a fisherman, and he would tell us stories about the ocean, about the things that happened to him when he was out on the water … and the things he'd seen. 'There are devils that live in the sea,' he'd say. 'They make their home in the darkest waters, places where no sunlight can reach. Most of the time they stay there and are no bother to us. But sometimes a thing attracts their attention and draws them to the surface. When that happens, it is best to remain on land and away from the water's edge.'"

Abuela told him more tales of these sea devils – always when Mami wasn't around to hear, of course – and he loved them all, the scarier the better. But as he grew older, he began to view

Abuela's stories in much the same way Mami did, as simple folklore, at best cautionary tales to encourage children to be safe in the water, or at worst as the foolishness of uneducated people.

Then one day, in the summer of his fifteenth year, he went to the beach with a group of friends, including Maria, a beautiful raven-haired girl he desperately wanted to impress. But so did the other boys. They all acted like clowns, boasting, making jokes, being loud, wrestling, doing handstands, whatever they could to get her attention. It was Tomas who suggested a competition to see who could hold his breath the longest. They were to swim out a ways, dive down, and stay under for as long as they could. The last one to surface would be the winner.

In his memory, Maria had stood on the beach watching, enthralled by the boys' daring – by *his* daring. But as an adult, he realized that she had probably been laughing inside at their stupidity, and he didn't blame her in the slightest.

Seven boys took part in the competition. They lined up on the beach and waited for Maria to give the signal for them to start. She held her hand above her head, and then brought it swiftly down, simultaneously shouting, "Go!"

The boys ran all out, each trying to be the first to reach the water. Roberto got there first – he'd always been the fastest – but Tomas was a close second. The water was colder than he'd expected, and it came as a shock as he dove into it. But he quickly adjusted as he swam, warmed by his body's exertions. When the boys were fifty feet from shore, they stopped, and turned back to face the girls – to face Maria. Once more she held her hand high, and when she brought it down, the boys drew in a huge breath of air, and then sank beneath the waves.

Tomas loved the water, and he felt a peaceful calm envelop him as he floated in its embrace. He moved his hands and feet in small motions to keep himself in place without exerting himself too much – the better to conserve oxygen – and he closed his eyes and concentrated on relaxing his body in order to slow the beat of his heart. He didn't bother counting the seconds he remained underwater. Doing so would only make him feel increasingly tense, which in turn would use up his oxygen supply faster. Instead, he imagined that time wasn't passing at all, that he was suspended in a single moment that stretched on and on. It was easy enough to do. The ocean was eternal, and when you were held within its grasp, time ceased to have any meaning. He would stay this way, existing in what was almost a state of altered consciousness, until his lungs were empty and aching for air, and then he would stay a bit longer after that before finally surrendering to the inevitable and kicking back toward the surface. Would he emerge the victor? He thought he might. And if not … at least he would have had a few wonderful moments when he felt as one with the infinite.

He didn't know what made him open his eyes. Maybe the current flowed around his body in a different way, or maybe there was some subtle sound, one that only registered subconsciously. Or maybe it was some primal instinct that warned him he was no longer alone in the water. Whichever the case, he opened his eyes and found himself staring into the face of a bull shark. The animal was less than five feet away and gliding toward him, gray-bodied with a pale underside, and a blunt, rounded snout. No teeth were visible – this wasn't some cartoon shark with oversized jutting teeth – but Tomas didn't need to see the teeth to know they were there and what they could do to his flesh.

Cold panic stabbed Tomas' gut, and his heart began pounding in his ears trip-hammer fast. He almost released the air stored in his lungs in a terrified shout, but he managed to keep himself from doing so, more from fear of doing anything that might cause the shark to attack than out of concern for winning some stupid contest. The shark continued its approach, seeming to move so slowly that Tomas thought this was the kind of thing people talked about when they said time seemed to stand still, like when they were in a car crash or standing at a teller's window when a bank robbery occurred. He tried to think of what you were supposed to do when you encountered a shark, but his mind came up blank. All he could do was watch as death approached.

His Abuela's words came back to him then. *There are devils that live in the sea.*

The shark – which he estimated was close to ten feet in length – drew within two feet before veering off to the left. As it passed, Tomas looked into its eye and saw only darkness there, so absolute, so profoundly *nothing*, that he knew at once what this creature truly was. It might wear the shape of a bull shark, but in truth it was one of Abuela's sea devils, and he and his friends had made the mistake of drawing its attention with their foolish competition. Why the shark turned away at the last moment before attacking, Tomas didn't know, nor did he particularly care. He kicked toward the surface, burst into the air, and began swimming for shore as fast as he could, all the while expecting to feel the sharp teeth of the sea devil clamping down on his legs. But he didn't, and he reached shore safely.

He lost the contest, was in fact the first boy to rise for air, but he didn't tell anyone what had caused him to return to shore. He was too embarrassed, and he didn't want Maria to think he was an immature boy who believed in an old woman's silly stories. He feared she already thought of him as a loser. Roberto won the contest – of course – and he won Maria. For that summer, at least. By the time school started, they'd already broken up and were dating other people. Tomas never asked Maria out, never even spoke to her again. Maybe because he couldn't bear the thought of her laughing at him for how fast he'd swam back to shore that day. Or maybe because somewhere in his mind, he associated her with his encounter with the sea devil. Whichever the case, he hadn't seen her for nearly twenty years. Last he'd heard, she was an audiologist working at a hospital in Atlanta.

"So what exactly *are* these things we're looking for?"

Taylor's voice brought him back to the here and now.

"Fuck if I know," he said. But that wasn't true, was it? He knew precisely what these creatures were. Whatever they might appear to be on the outside, inside they were sea devils, and a part of him that was still fifteen couldn't help wondering if they'd come to finish the job their companion had failed to do on that long-ago day.

Let them try, he thought, and unconsciously patted the Beretta on his hip.

He decided it was time to check in with the other teams and see how they were doing. But as he reached for his walkie-talkie, the water in front of the bow exploded in a shower of white froth, and a sleek dark form shot toward the boat.

CHAPTER TEN

Just as when the bull shark came at Tomas, time seemed to slow to a crawl. He saw the thing's crocodile-like head, its open jaws, the twin rows of sharp white teeth. The size of the thing didn't surprise him as much as its mass. The creature had to be close to fifteen feet long, but its body appeared to be all muscle beneath the mottled, scaled hide. It had to be strong as hell to launch itself out of the water like this, and he thought of nature documentaries he'd seen showing great white sharks leaping into the air, executing a flip like some kind of trained animal, and then plunging back down into the ocean. It was this display of strength, even more than its size, that told Tomas this creature was a formidable foe.

And then he saw the thing's eyes – or rather, *eye*, for it had only one – and in the triangular pupil, he saw the same darkness that he'd seen within the bull shark's, and he knew the sea devils hadn't spared him. They'd only given him a reprieve, allowed him to believe he was safe for all these years, and now they'd come for him at last in the guise of these monsters.

Despite these thoughts, he was no longer a frightened boy. His marine training kicked in, and he reached for his gun. But before he could draw it, the creature landed on the bow of the runabout with a jarring thump. Its narrow snout broke through the windshield, and its head turned to the side so it could fasten its jaws around Taylor's neck. Tomas heard a sickening crunch and Taylor's head popped off her neck in a spray of blood and flew out of the boat and hit the water with a *ker-plunk*. The impact of the creature's landing knocked Tomas off his feet and he fell onto the deck. He lost his grip on the Beretta as he hit, and it skittered away. Blood rained down on him from Taylor's neck as the animal – it looked like some kind of fucking dinosaur – gnawed at the ragged stump. Her body jerked and shuddered, still held upright by the monster's jaws.

Without a pilot, the runabout swung hard to starboard and ran aground on the bank. The boat hadn't been traveling very fast, but even so, it slid along the grass for several feet before listing to port, dumping Tomas and Taylor's headless body onto the ground. The creature landed on its back less than five feet from where Tomas lay on his stomach, arms out before him, head raised. Its jaws snap-snapped-snapped as it thrashed around in a frantic attempt to right itself and get its teeth on Tomas or Taylor. Tomas didn't think it mattered to the goddamned thing which one of them it ate, or whether its meal was alive or dead, just as long as if could put something in its belly *now*.

Tomas was mesmerized by the sight of the thing, and for several seconds, he lay there gazing at the monster in stunned fascination, but then the marine in Tomas shouted for him to get control of himself if he didn't want to end up as this fucker's next bowel movement. He moved into a crouching position and cast his gaze about for something, anything he could use as a weapon. The Beretta had fallen out of the boat and lay on the bank less than ten feet from where he crouched, and he sent a quick prayer of thanks to God for this small bit of luck. The sea devil was closer to the gun, its head less than a yard away from it, and if the beast managed to flip over before Tomas could reach the weapon, there was an excellent chance it would lunge forward and fasten its teeth onto his flesh before he could grab hold of the gun, let alone get off a shot.

Of course, he could simply move farther up the bank and be well out of the devil's reach. When the thing righted itself and saw its prey had escaped, it would return to the water – probably dragging Taylor's corpse with it – and swim off, leaving Tomas behind, safe and uninjured. But he didn't flee, even though he knew it would've been the wisest choice. He was aware of people standing at the railings on either side of the bank, watching – and recording – in horrified fascination. But he wasn't the kind of man who cared what other people thought of him. So what if they saw and recorded him scuttling up the bank to avoid the monster's jaws? So what if they, and perhaps the whole world, thought him a coward for doing so? Their opinion meant nothing to him. But his opinion of himself … well, that *did* matter. Mattered very much indeed. The monster had killed Taylor, had torn off her head as easily as a child could pull the wings off a fly. He couldn't let that go unanswered. Besides, he was Elysium's head of security. It was his job to protect everyone on the island, and once he took on a job, he saw it through to the end, to hell with the consequences.

He sprung to his feet and ran toward the gun. The sea devil twisted its body again, and this time, it was successful. It flopped over onto its white belly when Tomas was only halfway to the Beretta. The devil made a grunting sound and pushed its body toward him using all four flippers, extending its neck to its full length, jaws snapping. When Tomas was within a few feet of the gun, he dove for it, just in time to prevent the devil from getting its teeth on his left leg. He hit the ground, rolled, and came up with the Beretta in his hand. He pointed it at the monster's head, aiming for the spot directly between its eyes – or rather, one eye and one hollow socket – and fired.

He expected the bullet to penetrate the beast's skull in a spray of blood. But instead, the round ricocheted off the devil's thick hide without so much as leaving a dent. The impact must've hurt like blazes, though, for the devil turned and began making its way toward the water, moving surprisingly fast for a large creature that wasn't designed to operate on land.

Tomas continued firing at the thing, hoping to find a weak point somewhere on its body. Most of the rounds proved no more effective than the first, but one struck the area directly behind the right rear flipper, and Tomas was elated to see blood spurt from a newly created wound. It made sense that the animal's vulnerable areas would be around its flippers, for they needed to be free to move, and being surrounded by armored hide would restrict their movements too much.

He expected the devil to let forth a cry of pain, but all it did was release a soft hiss. It gave a mighty heave with its three uninjured flippers and propelled itself the last couple feet to the water. It slipped into the canal, entering the water without a splash and leaving only a few ripples behind to mark its passing. That, and a trail of blood.

* * * * *

One-Eye moved down the canal as fast as he could with only three working flippers. The bullet that had hit him hadn't gone deep, but it had done enough damage to render that flipper almost useless. He had no concept of weapons, of course, but he understood pain, understood it *very* well, and he knew that the soft skins – which were quite tasty – could bite back when they wanted.

The injury didn't concern him overmuch. When you lived in the Great Deep, injury was an ever-present risk, even for creatures as strong and deadly as his kind were. But displaying weakness of any kind to the others in his pod … *that* was dangerous. He was dominant among the nestlings. At least he had been until this injury, and all of them would view his current weakness as an opportunity to unseat him and take his place in the pod's hierarchy. Especially his brother. He knew Brokejaw was close. The two of them always hunted together, had since the day of their hatching. Several years ago, One-Eye had been attacked by an overly ambitious tiger shark. He'd bested his opponent and devoured it, but not before losing an eye – and gaining a new name. Brokejaw had challenged him then, but he'd fought off his brother's attack easily, severely wounding him in the process and giving *him* a new name. But losing an eye was nothing compared to losing the use of a flipper, and he needed to put distance between himself and his brother before Brokejaw –

He felt a vibration in the water off to his right, the side where his bad eye was, and he veered left just in time to evade Brokejaw's strike. Brokejaw had intended to take hold of his brother's injured flipper and tear it off, reducing his ability to maneuver enough so Brokejaw could finally kill his brother and take his place. And when the next mating season came around, he would mate with both Nub and Whiteback, and his genes, not his brother's, would be carried into the future.

But even wounded, One-Eye was far from easy prey.

One-Eye swung back toward Brokejaw as he passed and rammed his snout into his brother's chest. Bubbles burst forth from Brokejaw's mouth as the air was forced out of his lungs, and he instinctively headed toward the surface to refill them. One-Eye didn't take advantage of the opportunity for a follow-up attack.

He might still have all four of his flippers, but injured as he was, there was no way he could outmaneuver Brokejaw forever. Best to flee and regain his strength so he would be ready should Brokejaw attempt to challenge him again. One-Eye wasn't human – he had no pride and he felt no shame at fleeing. In many ways, his kind were little more than simple machines. Kill, eat, fuck, and swim so they could continue to kill, eat, fuck, and swim – this comprised the entirety of their programming. One-Eye did not view himself as running away, had not the first notion of the concept. He was *surviving*, and right now, that was all that mattered.

So he swam off as fast as he could, doing his best to ignore the pain of his wound as he surged through the water like a wobbly torpedo.

* * * * *

Brokejaw raised his snout above the water's surface just enough so he could draw in air and no further. It was the way of his kind, a way which had helped them remain hidden from prey – and from those who would prey upon them – since the time of their ancestors. So while dozens of people were gathered around the canal fences, none of them saw him. They were too busy talking about the attack they had witnessed and watching the security guard who'd driven off the monster who'd killed his partner. He was scanning the water, gun held out before him, waiting for another attack. But he didn't see Brokejaw's nostrils either, or else he would've started shooting.

When Brokejaw's lungs were full again, he descended once more. One-Eye had left a trail of blood, and Brokejaw knew he could use it to track his brother. But just as One-Eye had no pride or shame, Brokejaw had no need for revenge. He'd attacked his brother solely out of instinct, and now that One-Eye was gone, there was nothing to trigger that instinct again. Brokejaw's chest still throbbed from where One-Eye had rammed him. He felt no resentment toward his brother for causing this pain, though, for just like him, One-Eye had only acted out of instinct.

Now Brokejaw's instincts told him to rejoin his brother. While his kind could hunt alone – and sometimes did, as when One-Eye had attacked the humans' boat – they preferred to hunt in pairs. So Brokejaw followed slowly after his brother, intending only to hunt by his side once more. But when he caught up with One-Eye and saw he was still injured … well, what he did then would all depend on what his instincts told him at the time, wouldn't it?

CHAPTER ELEVEN

Joel thought he'd have a tough time convincing the money people at the network to pony up the cash for a trip to *Las Dagas* for him and his crew. But after seeing the video of the monsters attacking the two women, the network reps were only too thrilled to foot the bill. They were already planning a special two-hour event episode of *The Hidden World* focusing on the creatures, whatever the hell they were. So Joel, Pam, and Owen hauled ass to the nearest airport in Cincinnati, got on the flight the network had arranged for them – not first class, but Joel supposed you couldn't have everything – and off they went. After a blessedly short layover at LAX, they arrived in Nicaragua ten hours later. The network had arranged for them to be flown to the island via helicopter, and soon after that, they landed. It was after midnight local time, and while the three of them had managed to get some sleep during their flights, by the time they reached the Crescent Hotel, they were exhausted. Joel had brought a shitload of caffeine pills and tried to get Pam and Owen to take some with him so they could get to work right away, but he couldn't talk them into it.

We'll get started tomorrow at eight a.m., Pam had said. *No earlier.* And from the tone in her voice, Joel had known she meant it. *We have a meeting with the resort's executive manager then, remember?*

Joel and Owen shared a room while Pam had one to herself. Being a producer, even of a crappy cable show, had its perks. Joel had refrained from taking any caffeine pills, but once he was in bed – Owen on the other one, snoring softly – he found he was too wired to sleep. So while Owen and Pam got their Z's, he turned on his tablet computer, connected to the hotel's Wi-Fi, and checked the Net to see what had happened on *Las Dagas* while they'd been traveling. A security officer had been killed by one of the creatures, and multiple videos of the incident had been uploaded to the web, and Joel watched them all. This time, the creature – one of the ones from the first video, he thought – ended up on the canal bank, giving the world its first really good look at it. He took screen shots of the thing and studied them closely, and he agreed with a lot of the people who commented on the videos that the animal was some kind of aquatic dinosaur. What the hell else *could* it be? Although he hated seeing such a unique and special creature get hurt, he couldn't help being impressed by the surviving security officer who remained to fight the dinosaur instead of running away. The guy was a genuine badass.

Joel had been nine when his parents had taken him on a cruise to Hawaii, and he'd been so excited. It felt like he was going on a real adventure, but the reality proved to be disappointingly mundane. This particular cruise wasn't kid-friendly, so there hadn't been much for him to do, and he couldn't find anyone his own age to hang out with. His brother Johnny was six years older than he was, and he didn't really like to play with Joel. He hadn't even come on the cruise, opting instead to stay with their grandparents. So one afternoon, bored out of his mind, Joel was standing at the ship's railing, looking out over the water when he'd seen it: a huge marine reptile of some sort, at least fifty feet long, swimming alongside the ship. Joel watched in astonishment as the creature swam close, nudged the hull with its snout, and then – as if deciding the ship wasn't good to eat – submerged. Almost frantic with excited, he'd ran to tell his parents. They'd listened quietly and then immediately took him to see the ship's doctor.

When he finished viewing the videos, pouring over the images he'd saved, and reading online comments from scientists and Joe and Jane Average, he had no doubt that the creatures that had invaded *Las Dagas* were the same species as the thing he'd seen so long ago, the thing that had started his lifelong search for cryptids. And now it looked like he'd finally found one at last. His holy fucking grail.

The network had sent Joel some emails, messages that had also been sent to Pam and Roy. The Lexana Corporation had temporarily halted all travel to the island. Partially because they didn't want to be responsible for any thrill-seekers who might come looking to get a peek at the *Las Dagas* Monsters, as they'd been dubbed, but also because reporters from all around the world were desperate to come to the island to film on-the-scene reports. The only travel currently permitted was for those guests and employees who wanted to get the hell off the island before they ended up as monster chow.

Given the prohibition on incoming travelers, Joel was surprised that he and his team had been allowed to land on *Las Dagas*, until he read that several of the board members watched his show. Or at least their children and grandchildren did. *Never know where you'll find a fan,* Joel thought.

The board had released a single statement confirming that a pair of guests had been attacked and killed by animals of unknown origin, but which were suspected to be a rare species of saltwater crocodile. As for the videos posted online purporting to show attacks by creatures that appeared to be something quite different than crocodiles, the board's only comment was, essentially, that you can't believe everything you see on the Internet.

Horseshit, Joel thought.

He supposed the board might have had an ulterior motive for allowing him and his crew to come. If Lexana hoped to downplay these attacks, maybe even discredit the videos posted online, what better way to do it than by having a cable TV show about hunting cryptids be the only reporting permitted about the creatures? Nothing about *The Hidden World* was fake. Joel, Pam, and Owen made damn sure of that. But to most people, even a good portion of their viewers, their show was just entertaining bullshit, not to be taken seriously. Having the *Las Dagas* Monsters featured on *The Hidden World* could, in the end, prove more effective at helping the board mitigate the bad publicity generated by the uploaded videos of the attacks by causing people around the world to begin doubting they were authentic.

Maybe he was being paranoid. Maybe he wasn't. Either way, he didn't care. All that mattered was that he was here, and that he, Pam, and Owen were scheduled to meet with the resort's executive director tomorrow morning for an "exclusive interview." And after that? Well, with any luck, they'd get some footage of the *Las Dagas* Monsters in action. Real footage, not some shaky, blurry amateur video. And then at least one small part of the hidden world would be hidden no longer.

And with that thought, he closed his eyes and fell asleep, head leaning back against the headboard. His fingers accidentally touched the tablet's screen and started a video of the monster killing the security officer – its teeth severing her head as easily as a person biting off a soft piece of banana. The video continued playing on a loop while Joel slept, and as the woman was decapitated over and over, he dreamed.

* * * * *

Joel is nine years old, and he's standing at the ship's railing, looking out over the ocean, feeling wind against his face, riffling his hair, smelling saltwater, and marveling at the way sunlight glitters on the ocean surface like an endless scatter of diamonds. He's never seen anything so beautiful in his short life, never felt anything this intensely, and he wishes time would freeze right now, so he could remain in this one perfect moment forever.

And that's when he sees it, a huge rounded mass, mottled gray and black, rising from the water only a few dozen yards from the ship. At first, he thinks it's an island, forced to the surface by some kind of underwater volcano or seismic activity on the ocean floor. He saw a movie like that once – *Raiders from the Deep* – where an island filled with bloodthirsty fish people was brought to the surface by an earthquake. But this doesn't look like an island. It's smooth, with the exception of a protruding ridge running down the middle, bisecting it. He realizes then that he's looking at *skin*. An instant later, his realization is confirmed when a reptilian head breaks the surface. Its long tapering snout is filled with teeth, and as he watches in fascinated horror, the monster turns and begins swimming toward the ship, slowly at first but with increasing speed.

Joel can't estimate the size of the thing. All he knows is that it's *big*. Not as big as the ship, but maybe half that size. But as terrifying as the creature is, it's nothing compared to what Joel sees next. A second creature, equally as large as the first, comes to the surface. It's followed by a third, then a fourth, and then there are a dozen. Two dozen. All gigantic, all heading toward the ship, churning the water to white froth as they come.

Joel grips the railing as the monsters come, wanting to flee but unable to make his body move. A part of him realizes he's gotten his earlier wish. In a sense, time *has* frozen for him. And then the first of the behemoths slam into the ship's hull. He hears a loud *throom*, as if something deep inside the ship has exploded, and he feels the metal railing shudder against his hands, feels the deck vibrate beneath his feet. Before he can retreat, the monsters begin striking the ship one after the other. *Throom throom, throom!* And although he can't see it, he knows that the monsters aren't only attacking this side of the ship. They're attacking from all sides, throwing themselves against the hull again and again.

They want to break the ship apart, he thinks, *like they're trying to open a can to get at the food inside.*

The ship lurches back and forth now, and he holds onto the railing for dear life. People run across the deck, yelling and screaming, and he calls out for his mommy and daddy, tears running down his face, but they do not come. He has no idea where they are, whether or not they're safe. He only knows they aren't here.

The impacts against the hull grow louder, the vibrations juddering through the ship more intensely. He can see that the monsters are now coordinating their attacks, three or four working together to strike the same point on the hull and maximize the damage they cause. Are these things intelligent enough to work in teams? It seems impossible, but that's what he's seeing. He tells himself that he needs to get away from the railing, He doesn't know if any place on the ship is safe by this point, but he knows standing here at the railing isn't it. He needs to release his death-grip on the railing and go in search of whatever shelter he can find, but while his mind understands the logic of this, his body believes that the wisest course of action is remaining where he is and doing nothing to draw attention to himself.

Come on, you can do it, he tells himself. *One hand at a time.*

He starts with the left hand, concentrates on relaxing his grip and letting his fingers fall away from the metal railing. At first, nothing happens, and he feels a stab of fear that he won't be able to do it, that he'll be stuck standing here, holding onto the damn railing as the ship sinks. But then his left hand slips away from the railing and falls limply at his side.

One down.

The monsters continue battering the ship. *Throom, throom, throom!*

He focuses his attention on his right hand and tries to repeat the process. But just as the fingers begin to relax, there's an especially strong impact against the hull. *THROOM!* He pitches forward over the railing, and although he now desperately tries to hold onto it, his left hand slips away, and he plunges downward.

Once again, time seems to freeze for him, or at least slow down, and he sees one of the monsters is positioned directly beneath him, head tilted upward, mouth wide open, ready to receive the tender little morsel that is rapidly descending.

Joel screams as he falls. Unable to close his eyes, he watches as the mouth grows closer … closer … closer … And then he plunges past the teeth and into the darkness beyond.

* * * * *

"Fuck!"

Joel sat up in bed, covered with sweat and shaking as if in the throes of a deadly fever. He had trouble breathing at first, so he concentrated on taking one breath after another. In … out. In … out. As his shaking subsided, he saw the video of the two women being killed was still playing on his tablet. He shut it off and looked over at Owen. The cameraman remained sound asleep, still snoring lightly. Joel was glad he hadn't awakened Owen, mostly because he didn't want to have to explain his nightmare to the man.

He'd dreamed variations of the monsters-attack-the-cruise-ship scenario over the years. Sometimes the ship sank. Sometimes it only sank halfway and the monsters leaped onto the deck and began eating people. Sometimes the monsters – which were much larger in his dreams than the one he'd seen in real life – burst upward through the deck. But out of all the versions of the nightmares, the one he hated most was when he was knocked over the railing and plummeted into the open mouth of one of the monsters. He hadn't had that one for a while, and it didn't take a degree in psychology to figure out that this version had returned because he was on *Las Dagas*, where the monsters from his nightmares were all too real, if diminished in stature. It occurred to him then that it was now possible for his nightmares to come true. He could get eaten by one of the monsters if he wasn't careful.

He'd been fascinated by cryptids even since the day he'd spotted the sea monster from the deck of the ship, and he'd made the search for such creatures his life's work. But despite how seriously he'd taken his quest, he'd never once considered the possibility that it could end up killing him.

Shit, as they say, had just got real.

CHAPTER TWELVE

Ysmin decided to hold the meeting in the Crescent's staff lounge rather than in her office. For one thing, there wasn't enough room there. But she also didn't want to deal with what she'd come to think of as "the Situation" in her office because it felt like a sanctuary to her, a place where she could go to escape the pressures of her job when she needed to, one of those escapes being screwing Tomas' brains out from time to time. She didn't want this nightmare intruding on her personal space any more than necessary.

There wasn't much to the lounge – round wooden tables with plastic and metal chairs, several vending machines lined up against one wall, a picture window with a view of the ocean … Before yesterday, she'd thought the view lovely. Now all she could think about was how many of those damn monsters might be out there, concealed by the water.

Coffee and pastries had been provided for everyone. This *was* a hotel, after all.

She sat at one of the tables near the doorway, Tomas standing at her side. He'd told her about his encounter with one of the monsters yesterday. More, she'd seen the videos witnesses had posted online. She'd been both horrified and aroused to see Tomas fight the monster, and she was looking forward to getting him alone so she could show him how much she appreciated his dedication to his job. But first, she had a crisis to deal with.

"Before we get started, I think it would be useful if we went around the room and introduced ourselves," she said.

Andrew Rivera – the marine biologist who sat with his daughter Lara, both of whom had arrived on the island yesterday afternoon – glared at the cable TV reporter. If a term like *reporter* could be applied to someone who spent his life chasing imaginary creatures.

"Lara and I are already acquainted with Mr. Tucker," Andrew said, his cold tone indicating that such acquaintanceship had been less than positive.

From the way Joel and Lara kept glancing at one another when they thought the other wasn't looking, Ysmin figured they had been involved at some point. Joel must've initiated the breakup or done something to cause Lara to break up with him. No other reason for a father to glare at an ex-boyfriend of his daughter's like that.

Joel sighed and nodded. "Yeah, we know each other." He gestured to the man and woman sitting with him. "This is my producer Pam Powell and our cameraman Owen Rogers."

"Well, *I* don't know who any of you are or why you're here."

This was said by a man sitting alone at a table, arms crossed and looking at the others with suspicious wariness. He needed no introduction as he had one of the most recognizable faces in the world.

Andrew turned to glare at Shayne Ferreira. He was really good at glaring, Ysmin thought.

"And I want to know why the hell a third-rate star of gross-out comedies is suddenly interested in marine science," he said.

Shayne's face turned an angry red. "Third-rate?" He practically spit out the words as if they were poisonous.

"Don't be insulted," Andrew said. "At least you're not a popularizer of the worst sort of pseudoscience." He turned his glare back on Joel. Lara put her hand on her father's arm as if attempting to calm him down, but he didn't seem to notice.

Joel pointedly refused to look at Andrew, but Pam and Owen glared back at him. Pam looked so angry, Ysmin wouldn't have been surprised if the woman jumped up from her table and punched Andrew in his wrinkly testicles.

Ysmin briefly considered walking out of the lounge, going to her office, calling someone on the board, and tendering her resignation. She definitely didn't need to deal with this sort of bullshit right now. But Tomas put a hand on her shoulder and gave it a gentle squeeze, as if to say, *Steady on*, and she took a deep breath and continued.

"Let's move on. As you may or may not be aware, Elysium's parent corporation is attempting to downplay the more … sensational aspects of the attacks."

"You mean covering them up," Joel said.

"Not at all. They know the full truth will get out sooner rather than later. In fact, they're counting on it."

"They want to make a profit off the monsters," Shayne said. "Maybe even turn this place into a mini version of *Jurassic Park*. Smart business move."

Ysmin didn't bother to confirm Shayne's theory, but neither did she see any point in denying it.

"They hope to get the situation here under control – without any further loss of life – before the world's media descends upon the island like a flock of vultures on a freshly dead carcass."

"They don't want to risk control," Lara said. "Or having anyone else capture one of the creatures."

Again, Ysmin saw no need to confirm or deny.

"At first, they wanted Tomas and I to handle everything ourselves. But when you arrived –" She looked at Andrew and Lara – "I realized you could be of great help to us. I informed the board that you were here and they instructed me to allow you to aid us as we attempt to resolve our problem."

"*Allow?*" Andrew said, indignant. "I've been studying these creatures for most of my life! I've lost all shred of academic credibility because of it! My wife –" He broke off then, eyes glistening. For a moment, Ysmin thought he might cry, but then he said, "You're lucky *I'm* allowing you to work with *me*." And then he fell silent.

There's a story there, Ysmin thought, but she wasn't sure it was one she wanted to hear. She faced Joel and his companions. "The board of directors informed me that the three of you were coming and that they wished me to cooperate with you as well."

What she didn't say was the board wanted *The Hidden World* to cover this story because they thought it would be easier to exert influence on a small-time cable show than a major news network, and thus they could craft the coverage to their liking. Ysmin wasn't certain this was a good idea, though. From what she understood of Joel Tucker, he was a true believer in his cause:

revealing the truth about cryptids to the world. In her experience, true believers – whatever the nature of their belief – were difficult if not impossible to control.

"What about Shayne?" Joel asked. He glanced at the man then looked back at Ysmin. "No offense, but I don't see what he brings to the table. Andrew and Lara are both scientists, and Andrew's an expert in the type of creature that I believe has come to *Las Dagas*. Pam, Owen, and I chase monsters for a living. But Shayne …"

"He stars in fart-and-fuck comedies," Owen finished. He look at Shayne and grinned. "Don't get me wrong. I *love* your movies. They're funny as hell."

Shayne acknowledged Owen's praise with a strained smiled.

Ysmin couldn't tell the others the truth, that Shayne was here because he'd threatened to release the video he'd taken of Echo Amato being killed by one of the monsters.

You've seen the reaction to the other videos, he'd said when he'd come into her office yesterday. *Imagine what would happen if the public saw video of one of the most beloved pop stars in the world being eaten by one of those toothy fuckers?*

Shayne's price for his silence? Whatever sort of investigation there was going to be into these monsters, whatever kind of plan Ysmin and Tomas would come up with for dealing with them, he wanted in on it. *In on the action,* he'd said, putting a slight emphasis on the last word, as if it held some special meaning for him. Simply put, Shayne was here because he was blackmailing her, but she couldn't tell the others that. But before she could come up with some bullshit excuse, Shayne spoke once more.

"When the board found out I was staying on the island, they asked me to get involved. They feel that my celebrity might be useful in helping with the PR aspect of this mess. It doesn't hurt that I'm a comic, either. Not that I'd ever treat what's happening here as funny," he hastened to add. "But people associate me with humor. Something positive, you know?"

As lies went, Ysmin thought this one wasn't half-bad. Shayne would've done well in the corporate world. She looked at the others to see if they bought Shayne's story, and while none of them looked especially convinced, none questioned his explanation, and she took that as a sign to keep the meeting moving.

"Our plan is simple," Ysmin said. "The Doctors Rivera will handle the scientific aspect of the investigation, Joel and his friends will document their work, and Tomas and his people will concentrate on keeping those guests who've chosen to remain on the island safe."

Andrew gave Tomas a suspicious look. "You're not planning on killing the animals, are you? They're too valuable to science."

Tomas replied calmly. "If you're asking if we're going to out on a monster hunt with the express intent to kill them, the answer is no." He glanced at Ysmin. "The board made its wishes clear on this matter. But if there's another attack by those devils and one of my people is present, they have orders to do whatever is necessary to protect human life, theirs or anyone else's."

Andrew looked as if he might object to this, but Lara put one of her hands over his, and he looked at her, nodded, and remained silent.

From the research Ysmin had conducted since Andrew's arrival, the scientific community considered him to be a delusional has-been. Now professional redemption was within his grasp, and she wondered how far he'd go in order to obtain it.

Shayne spoke up then.

"I'd like to accompany Tomas if I could. It would be a great opportunity for me to see how someone like him deals with a situation like this. You know, research for future roles."

Tomas wasn't the easiest person to read. He maintained emotional control of himself at all times – with the exception of the bedroom, of course. But Ysmin knew him intimately on a number of levels, and she detected the slight furrowing of his brow and the almost imperceptible narrowing of his eyes. He did *not* want to be stuck playing nursemaid to a Hollywood actor looking to get some publicity for himself, but Ysmin had told him about Shayne's blackmail threat, and she knew he'd do whatever it took to protect Elysium.

"I would welcome that," Tomas said.

If Shayne noticed any lack of enthusiasm in Tomas' response, he didn't show it. He grinned like a child who'd just found a golden ticket in his Wonka bar.

Ysmin looked up at Tomas. "Could you tell everyone where things stand at the moment?"

Tomas gave her a brief nod before speaking.

"You are all aware of the videos that were uploaded to the Net. They show three people being killed by these devils. There has been one other death that we know of."

Thomas was too much of a professional to glance at Shayne, but Ysmin knew he was referring to Echo Amato. Ysmin noted his use of the word *devils* to describe the creatures, and she wondered if there was some reason for it. She'd ask him later.

He continued.

"There have been several reports of people missing – people who were swimming or boating – and while we have no proof they were killed by the creatures, that seems the most likely explanation."

"How many people are missing?" Pam asked.

Tomas hesitated a moment, as if reluctant to answer.

"Twelve."

Ysmin could see the shock on everyone's faces. Three people dead was a tragedy, but it really wasn't that many. No more than might die in an accident of some sort, like an automobile collision. It was – although she was certain none of them would think of it like this, let alone express it aloud – an *acceptable* number. But fifteen people total? That number was harder to accept.

"The canals are open to the ocean," Tomas said. "Normally, the entry points are covered by underwater fences made from PVC pipe."

"But the animals broke through," Andrew said.

"Yes, and not just in one place. All of the fences have been destroyed."

"They're traveling back and forth between the canals and the ocean," Andrew said. It wasn't a question.

"Do you think they'll leave?" Joel asked. "Return to the open ocean?"

Ysmin thought he sounded almost panicked at the possibility.

Andrew shot him a dark look, but he answered. "Unlikely. Something drew them to *Las Dagas*, and whatever that something is, it should keep them here a while yet."

Joel sat back in his chair, looking relieved. Ysmin found his response more than a bit ghoulish. The longer the creatures remained in the island's waters, the greater the chance that more people might die.

"The security staff and I have been patrolling the canals and the water around the island since we learned of the attacks. But aside from my own encounter with one of the devils yesterday, we've had no contact with them. Not so much as a sighting."

"That's only to be expected," Andrew said. "These aren't marine monsters – or *devils* – that kill wildly and indiscriminately. These are *animals*. Nothing more, nothing less. They kill to eat and, if necessary, in self-defense. They need time to digest their food. But they'll be hungry again eventually."

The man sounded almost excited by the prospect. Ysmin thought Andrew and Joel had more in common than either would care to admit.

"We don't have much in the way of weaponry," Tomas said. "Pistols and rifles primarily, and not a lot of them. This *is* a resort, after all. If I'd known we'd be attacked by *sea monsters* –" he gave Andrew a quick look – "I'd have stocked up on some serious armament."

Both Joel and Andrew seemed reassured by Tomas' words. Ysmin was seriously beginning to wonder about their priorities.

"The Riveras arrived yesterday," Ysmin said, "and they've already had the opportunity to investigate somewhat." She looked at Andrew and Lara. "Would you mind filling the rest of us in on what you know?"

"We *know* very little," Andrew said, a bit testily. "We can, however, hypothesize."

Ysmin gave him a frosty smile. "Then by all means do so."

The smile Andrew gave her in return was a self-satisfied one, and he rose to his feet, looking for all the world like a professor preparing to deliver a lecture to a class of particularly dense students.

"Allow me to begin by saying that I've only viewed the online videos. I've yet to see a living specimen up close. But based on what I've seen so far, I believe these creatures to be –"

"Pliosaurs," Joel interrupted.

Andrew gave him a look that said he'd gleefully strangle him if he thought he could get away with it. Then he turned away from Joel as if dismissing him and focused his attention on the others.

"Indeed. The animals are, as most of you know, my primary research interest, and I have long theorized that they may have survived into the present day. It seems I have been vindicated in that belief."

Before he could go on, Shayne said, "So these are some kind of dinosaurs, right?"

Lara answered instead of her father. "They're reptiles, not dinosaurs. In fact, they're distant cousins of modern-day turtles. They lived during the Triassic, Jurassic, and Cretaceous periods. They're believed to have gone extinct the same time that the dinosaurs did."

"Turtles?" Shayne said. "Are you shitting me?"

"Think sea turtles," Lara said. "Four flippers, armored backs …"

Shayne didn't look convinced, but he didn't argue.

"What sort of sounds do turtles make?" Tomas asked.

Lara looked surprised by his question. "Turtles don't have vocal cords, so they primarily grunt and hiss. Semi-aquatic ones chirp and click, too."

Tomas accepted her answer with a smile and a nod.

"So why did these turtlezillas suddenly show up here?" Owen asked. "And why now?"

"There could be several reasons," Andrew said. "*Las Dagas* could be located in what they consider to be their territorial waters."

"Elysium's construction took several years," Ysmin pointed out. "There were no sightings of the creatures during that time."

"Just because no one saw them doesn't mean they weren't here," Andrew said, a trifle smugly. "But there's another possibility. The island may be their spawning grounds."

Lara continued where her father left off. "Mother sea turtles can migrate thousands of miles to reach their breeding sites, and some species return to the place where they were hatched when it's their time to spawn."

"You're saying these pliosaurs came to the island to get their freak on?" Shayne asked.

"It's impossible to say for certain without empirical data," Andrew said. "But if I had to guess, that would be the theory I'd go with."

"If the pliosaurs breed in a similar fashion to sea turtles," Lara said, "the males and females have sex offshore and come ashore to lay their eggs."

"And since they traveled so far to get here," Andrew said, "they need to replenish the energy they expended."

"In other words, they need to eat a lot," Joel said.

Andrew didn't look at Joel as he replied. "Essentially."

"If they came here to lay their eggs, why haven't we seen them before?" Ysmin asked.

Lara shrugged. "They might not mate every year. Or they might nest in different locations from one year to the next."

"None of this matters," Tomas said. "Tell me what I need to know to do my job. Tell me how to protect people from them."

"That's obvious," Joel said. "Keep them away from the water. The pliosaurs might be able to come onto land, but they can't go very far and they aren't especially fast out of the water."

"Indeed," Andrew said. He still didn't look at Joel, but Ysmin thought she detected a slight softening in his tone.

Tomas scowled. Ysmin knew Joel's response to his question had irritated him, but he evidently decided to let it pass.

"How many of these things do you think there are?" Pam asked. "We've only seen two on the videos. The one that's missing and eye, and the one with the deformed mouth."

Andrew and Lara exchanged a look.

"We don't know," Lara said.

"There are at least four," Shayne said. His voice was flat, his face expressionless. "I saw a … friend attacked by two others. One was all white, and the other had both eyes and a normal jaw."

Ysmin thought either Andrew or Joel would press Shayne for more details, but they didn't. Maybe they sensed the pain behind Shayne's words and decided to let him be – for now.

"Let's hope four is all there is," Owen said. "In this case, more is definitely *not* merrier."

"The ones we've seen so far have been approximately fifteen feet long," Tomas said. "Is that as big as they get?"

"It's difficult to say for this species," Andrew said. "If we're right about the pliosaurs coming here to spawn, then they've reached sexual maturity. Sea turtles can take decades to reach the same point in their life cycle. So these could be adults that have reached their full growth."

"You said *could*," Ysmin pointed out.

"Fossil remains have been found of larger specimens," Lara said. "Some up to fifty feet long."

They all took a moment to digest that information. It was Shayne who finally broke the silence.

"If there are any that big, they won't be able to fit their fat asses into the canals, so that's something, right?"

"True," Ysmin said. But she was thinking about what Tomas had said earlier, about how a number of people swimming or boating had gone missing. That could be the work of the four pliosaurs they knew about. But there might be others in the waters surrounding the island, and they could be larger. Maybe *much* larger.

"So what's our next step?" Joel said. "What's the board expect us to do? Capture one alive?"

"If possible," Ysmin confirmed. "A dead body for study would also be acceptable."

Ysmin's guests exchanged looks with one another. Shayne seemed to answer for them all when he said, "Your board of directors is fucking crazy, you know that?"

CHAPTER THIRTEEN

They spent some more time discussing plans until they all agreed on a three-pronged course of action. Joel and his crew would accompany Andrew and Lara while they searched for signs of the pliosaurs on the island. Tomas would assign one of his people to act as their escort/protector. Thomas would continue patrolling the canals, and Shayne would accompany him to conduct his own "research." For her part, Ysmin would continue doing damage control, fielding calls and emails from board members and media representatives alike, and trying to keep a lid on this situation for as long as she could.

As she headed back to her office, she thought, *I'd rather be out there facing one of those monsters.*

* * * * *

Pam and Owen went to their rooms to get equipment and supplies for the day's filming, and Andrew spoke with Tomas in the hall about what he and Lara would require from the security staff to do his work. Shayne remained in the lounge, sitting at his table and talking to someone on his phone – his agent, Joel presumed – and Ysmin headed for her office. Lara still sat at her table, and Joel at his. She was pointedly not looking at him, but she hadn't gotten up and left, and he took that as an encouraging sign.

"Did you ever think we'd be here?" he asked.

For a moment, he thought she wasn't going to answer, but then she turned to him and said with mock-innocence, "You mean in Elysium?"

He smiled. "I mean this moment, when Andrew's theories are finally going to be proven correct."

Andrew Rivera had been something of a hero to Joel when he was growing up. After seeing the pliosaur on the cruise, he'd read everything about cryptids – especially sea monsters – that he could get his hands on. And Andrew's books had been among his favorites. *Unknown Fathoms, Ancient Waters,* and his all-time favorite, *They Still Hunt.* So when *The Hidden World* was picked up by the network, Joel had made it a priority to feature Andrew on an episode. That was how he'd gotten to meet his hero … *and* his hero's daughter. Joel had found Andrew harder to take in real life than he'd expected, which was something of a disappointment. But he and Lara had clicked right away. They'd started going out, and it looked like they were heading for a bonafide relationship. Joel had opened up to her and told her about his pliosaur sighting, and in turn, she told him about her mother's death – or least what Andrew told her about her death. While both she and her father had supposedly witnessed it, Lara claimed not to remember it. Joel had been stunned to learn how her mother had died. Andrew hadn't mentioned this in any book he'd written or interview he'd given. And that's when Joel fucked everything up.

That's amazing! he'd said. *Do you think Andrew would tell the story on camera?*

Lara had looked at him for a long moment – they'd been having coffee at a small café in Santa Monica – and then she'd gotten up and left without a word. They hadn't spoken since. He'd tried calling, texting, emailing but she never responded. He didn't blame her for walking out. He'd been an insensitive sonofabitch, concerned only about his stupid TV show.

"Honestly, I didn't," she said. "As much as I love Dad and support his work, I thought we'd never find a living pliosaur. Even if they still existed, there couldn't be very many of them left or someone would've found them by now. At least, that's what I told myself. But now …"

"Now they're real," Joel said.

She nodded.

"I want to say something before the others come back." He glanced over at Shayne and saw he was still absorbed in his phone conversation. Good. But before he could go on, Lara held up a hand to stop him.

"There's nothing to say. We're all here to do a job. My father wants to increase humanity's knowledge and reclaim his reputation in the process. You want to get better ratings."

With that, she rose from her table and walked into the hall to join her father and Tomas.

Joel sat there for a moment, feeling as if he'd been kicked in the balls and knowing he deserved it. He wasn't aware of Shayne walking over to him until the comedian clapped a hand on his shoulder.

"Man, that was *brutal*," he said.

Joel only sighed.

* * * * *

Lara wasn't happy that Joel and his crew were going to tag along on their investigation, but she decided not to protest. Not because she wanted to be near Joel – far from it – but because her father hadn't objected. Sure, outwardly he seemed pissed about Joel's inclusion, but she was Andrew Rivera's daughter, and she knew him better than anyone. He might not be Joel's biggest fan, but Joel offered something he couldn't resist: access to a public – and potentially worldwide – audience. What better way to reclaim his professional standing than by having his efforts on *Las Dagas* recorded? He was probably already imagining the profuse apologies he'd receive from the scientific establishment and how he'd rub their noses in his success.

I told you so, motherfuckers!

But of all those who'd doubted him, she'd been the one who'd hurt him the most. She'd never said anything to him, nor he to her, but she hadn't really believed pliosaurs still existed, and she was certain her father knew how she felt. If there was anyone he should say I told you so to, it was her.

Tomas had arranged for them to have the use of a runabout, along with one security officer to pilot it and a second armed with a rifle to protect them. That made for a total of seven people, a tight fit, but they'd manage. Andrew sat next to the pilot, a man named Sergio, with Lara squeezed in next to him. Their guard – a security officer named Tammy Chu – stood behind the pilot's seat, weapon held at the ready, head turning back and forth at regular intervals as she scanned the water for any hint of danger. She was a pretty Asian woman with short black hair, although not quite short enough to qualify as a military-style cut, and she wore the standard uniform for Elysium's security officers – blue short-sleeved shirt, shorts, and black running shoes. Joel, Pam, and Owen were behind her. Pam sat while Joel stood, one hand holding onto a railing to steady himself. Owen had a camera out and was recording, taking shots of the buildings, bridges, and people they passed. Right now, Owen was focusing on her father, who was gazing intently forward, eager for his first glimpse of the monster he'd been chasing for most of his life. They were headed to the scene of the first attack, near the resort's Grand Mall, where the two women had been killed. According to Andrew, if the pliosaurs had found food there once, there was a good chance they'd return to that same spot, looking for more.

She had no idea how Owen managed to stay on his feet given the runabout's motion. But he rarely needed to brace himself as he worked. Given the sort of places they went to on *The Hidden World,* she figured he'd had a lot of practice filming under challenging conditions. She wondered what her father would think if he knew she still watched Joel's program from time to time. More, she wondered what Joel would think. She felt an urge to turn and look at him, but she resisted. There was no way for her to do it without being obvious. Looking at him was one thing, but his *knowing* she was doing so was another matter entirely.

Before setting out, they'd debated the wisdom of traveling on the canals. After all, Tomas had been in a runabout with another security officer when one of the pliosaurs attacked, killing her, and nearly getting him, too. As Joel had pointed out in the meeting, the most effective way to protect yourself from a pliosaur attack was to stay away from the water. But the canals were the fastest way to travel around the island, and – as her father had argued – the water was where the animals were.

She'd thought maybe Joel, Pam, and Owen might object to being on the water, but to her surprise, they were excited by the prospect. *It's the only way to get the best shots,* Owen had said.

So here they were, all seven of them, motoring through Elysium's canal system, searching for monsters that would like nothing better than to sink their teeth into the humans' flesh and tear them apart.

Good times, she thought.

At first, she didn't understand why Pam was here. She'd always imagined producers working in offices, overseeing details like budgets while the creative people did the real work. And although Pam had been present when they did the show on her father, she hadn't paid much attention to her at the time. She'd been too busy watching Joel and starting to get interested in him. But now that she watched Pam more closely, she saw that she gave Owen instructions on what to shoot, and she collaborated with Joel on what he should say, how he should say it, and where and how he should stand while he did his thing. Lara had no idea if other producers were this involved, but Pam was, and her estimation of the woman went up several notches.

They approached a bridge, and a half dozen people – tourists, presumably – waved and cheered.

"Go get the bastards!" a man shouted.

"Fuck 'em up!" a woman yelled.

Her father shook his head as they passed under the bridge and continued on, leaving it, and their cheering section, behind.

"The pliosaurs are remarkable, certainly," Andrew said, "but they're still natural creatures. Why can't people understand that?"

But despite his words, there was a cold emptiness in his eyes, and she wondered if in his mind he was reliving her mother's death in a pliosaur's jaws. Maybe he kept saying pliosaurs were animals. But she wasn't sure if he truly believed it, not entirely, away. One some level, they had to be monsters to him, monsters that had killed his wife and the mother of his daughter. How could something like that ever be forgotten? She wondered which part of her father would come to the fore when he at last encountered a living pliosaur. The rational, distracted scientists or the long-grieving widower? And if it was the latter, what would that part of him do?

She was glad Tomas hadn't given Andrew a gun. She wasn't sure he could be trusted with one.

She turned to look out at the water before them, and wondered if, when a pliosaur finally showed itself to them, if she'd react any differently than her father might. Maybe it was a good thing she didn't have a gun either.

CHAPTER FOURTEEN

"Guys, I'm not sure this is a good idea."

Saanvi Bhatia stood on the canal bank thirty feet from the water's edge. Standing with her were her boyfriend Pete Lyons, her best friend Jenn Price, and Jenn's boyfriend, Aidan Runyun. They were all in their early twenties and had recently graduated from college, and to celebrate, they'd decided to come to Elysium before they became mired in the workaday world of jobs, bills, and taxes. Normally, poor recent graduates like themselves could never have afforded such an expensive trip. But Saanvi's parents were lawyers in Montreal – very successful ones – and they'd paid for both her and her friends to come here.

But as far as Saanvi was concerned, their dream vacation had turned into a nightmare the instant those two women had been killed. None of them had witnessed the attack – they'd been drinking at a small bar a couple miles away – but they'd received a text from a friend back home not long after, telling them they had to check out this sick video and providing a link. They'd all watched it, of course, but only Saanvi had been shocked by the monsters' savagery. Her friends, however, had found the video fascinating. They watched it multiple times, then watched other videos of the attack posted online. And when they were no longer enough, Pete had come up with the bright idea to visit the exact place where the women had been killed. Saanvi had thought it was morbid as hell, but the other three only laughed and told her to lighten the fuck up.

The girls wore light blouses, shorts, and flip-flops, while the boys were bare-chested and wore only shorts. All of them had their phones, of course. They'd no more go anywhere without them than they'd leave the house without their own heads. But the phones were important for what Pete had in mind.

"Come on," he said, slipping an arm around her waist and pulling her close. "This is going to make a *fantastic* video!"

"It sure as hell will," Aidan said. "It's going to kick major ass!"

"We *have* to do it," Jenn added. "I mean, we can't be here and *not* do it, you know?"

Saanvi didn't know anything of the kind. What she did know was that she'd been accepted by three different law schools, and she needed to make her choice as soon as possible. She intended to follow in her parents' footsteps and embark on a law career with a focus on business law. She had her future mapped out, and it didn't include taking foolish chances just to make a stupid video and upload it the Internet.

She pushed Pete away.

"This is as close as I'm going to get to the water, and if any of you give me shit about it, I'll turn around and head back to the hotel."

Pete looked at her for a moment, as if trying to gauge how serious she was. Finally, he held up his hands in surrender.

"Okay. No problem. Just don't make noise while we're recording, all right?"

He grinned and then turned and started toward the water. She didn't think he was pissed at her. Pete could be pushy when he wanted something, but overall, he was a fairly easygoing guy.

Aidan followed Pete, and Jenn gave her a disappointed look before trailing after the boys.

The plan was as simple as it was foolish. Jenn would record as Pete and Aidan went to the water's edge, explained to the audience – whoever they eventually might be – where they were and what had happened here. Afterward, the two idiots would get on their hands and knees and dunk their heads into the water to see who could remain underwater the longest, all while tempting the *Las Dagas* Monsters to come bite off the juicy morsels that were their heads.

Saanvi was surprised the scene of the double attack had been so easy to access. There was no police tape or barriers erected, no guards posted, not even any signs that said: DANGER! WATER INHABITED BY REALLY HUNGRY MONSTERS! But this wasn't Montreal, and she supposed they didn't have any real police here, just a bunch of rent-a-cops. Too bad. If there *had* been some guards present, then Pete's little production would've been halted before they began recording.

As Pete, Aidan, and Jenn got in place and prepared to start, Saanvi couldn't help feeling she'd abandoned her friends. Abandoned *Pete*, who she was pretty sure she loved and who she might marry if he asked her. After she graduated from law school, of course. Back at the hotel where they were staying, Pete had argued that the chances of an attack happening again in the same place were slim.

Whatever these damn things are, they don't live in the canals. They're too big. They're ocean animals that probably got into the canals by accident and were looking for a way out. You know, like a fly that gets trapped in your house that keeps bumping into a window because it thinks it can get out that way? They probably swam through the canals until they found one that dumped them back into the ocean again. And if any of them are still here, security is all over the water looking for them. I won't say what we want to do is completely risk-free, but then what in life is? Besides, the risk is what makes it fun.

He was probably right. The monsters probably *were* gone. At least they likely weren't hanging around here anymore. They'd probably gone back out to sea, where the food was more plentiful and didn't shoot at them.

She started walking toward Jenn, and when she reached her friend's side, Jenn gave her a smile and a thumbs-up. Saanvi smiled back and then looked at Pete. He grinned and mouthed, *Thank you.* She nodded, and then they began. Jenn started recording and pointed toward the boys to let them know they were good to go.

Pete spoke first.

"We're standing next to one of the canals in Elysium, the island resort where yesterday people were killed by some kind of a dinosaur or something." He held up his own phone and stepped closer to Jenn. "Check out the date on my phone. It's been almost two days since a pair of women were killed right here on the very spot where we're standing."

Aidan picked up the narration then.

"If you look around, you can see some of the same places that showed up in the video of their deaths."

Jenn slowly moved her phone from left to right, taking in the shops on the other side of the canal. When she was finished with this, she focused her camera back on the boys again, and Aidan continued.

"And if you look at the ground, you can see places where the women's blood was before the people who work here cleaned it up."

Jenn dutifully recorded video of bare patches of earth around them.

Pete spoke then. "My buddy and I are going to put our heads in the water – water that might at this moment conceal some kind of monster – and the first one of us that turns chickenshit and takes his head out loses."

He then turned to Aidan.

"Ready?" Pete asked.

"Always," Aidan answered.

The boys turned toward the water, got down on their hands and knees, then lowered their heads as if they were going to drink from the canal. But they kept lowering their heads until they noses almost touched the water. They took several deep breaths, then counted to three in unison and dunked their heads.

"This is *insane!*" Jenn said, forgetting Pete's admonition not to make any noise while they were recording.

The sight of Pete and Aidan's head under water made Saanvi nauseous. She wanted to look away, wanted to move back to where she'd been standing before. But she stayed where she was and continued watching. She'd been brought up agnostic, but now she said a silent prayer for the boys' safety. She told herself that if Pete came out of this safely, she'd ask him to marry her. *So come on, God, whoever or whatever you are. Help a girl out.*

Saanvi might have been the same age as her friends, but there were some things about them that she'd never understand, chief among them their near obsession with constantly posting on social media. Half the time, they only did the things they did so they'd have something new or weird to post. And they'd do crazy things – like stick their heads into a canal where ravenous sea monsters might be lurking. And all so a few dozen people would like the video when they uploaded it. It seemed like madness to her.

She continued watching Pete and Aidan, her anxiety mounting until it was close to full-blown panic. She had no idea how much time had passed since they'd submerged their heads. It seemed like hours. She couldn't take it anymore. She started toward the boys, ignoring Jenn's whispered protest as she walked in front of her camera. She planned to grab hold of Pete and Aidan's shorts and pull them back from the water. Then she would tell them that they were not only being stupid, they were being *suicidally* stupid. And if they were pissed at her for spoiling their fun, so what? At least they would be alive.

She stopped behind the boys, and although she was tempted to kick them both in the ass, she bent over and took hold of their shorts by the waist. She was about to pull them back when the water erupted in front of them. It happened too fast for many details to register on her mind. She had an impression of grayish-black skin, darkness-filled eyes, and lots and lots of teeth.

Pete and Aidan jerked as if something struck them hard, and Saanvi yanked them backwards so fast she fell on her ass. The sudden impact sent a jolt of pain up her spine, but she was scarcely aware of it. Pete and Aidan had landed on the bank, one on either side of her. But they weren't exactly intact.

Blood sprayed from ragged neck stumps of Pete and Aidan, falling on Saanvi like thick, warm rain, getting in her eyes and mouth. She tried to scream, but all she could manage was a gurgling sound. She turned her head to the side and coughed out of gout of crimson. Her stomach lurched, and she thought she would vomit, but she was able to hold it back. But something inside her mind broke – she could almost hear a snapping sound when it did – and a deep calm settled over her. Pete and Aidan were hurt, and she had to help them.

As she sat up, she was distantly aware that someone was screaming. Jenn probably. But she didn't look toward her to confirm it. She had to focus all her attention on the boys. She quickly looked from Pete to Aidan and back again and immediately saw that the problem was. The boys' heads were gone. She'd need to find them so doctors could reattach them, but first, she had to do something about their bleeding. She scooped her hands through the grass, attempting to gather as much blood as she could, then she slapped one hand over Pete's neck stump and the other over Aidan's, attempting to return the blood to their bodies. She had no way of knowing whose blood was whose – or if it was mixed together – but at this point, such details weren't important. She needed to get them stabilized before she could worry about anything else.

She continued this process, working frantically, knowing the boys didn't have much time. She was unaware of the tears streaming down her face, mixing with the blood coating her skin.

"Hang in there, guys. You're going to be fine."

She kept working while Jenn kept screaming.

CHAPTER FIFTEEN

Joel watched Owen recording video of Tammy. The woman continually scanned their surroundings, searching for signs of trouble and looking like she could handle anything that came her way. After a moment, Owen lowered his camera and stared at her, as if he wanted to see her without a lens getting in the way.

"Take a picture," Pam said. "It'll last longer."

For this first time since Joel had known Pam, she actually wore a short-sleeved shirt and shorts. She'd had to travel to South America to finally find a place warm enough for her.

"Hmm?" Owen looked at Tammy a moment more before turning to Pam and Joel and smiling with embarrassment. "Sorry. Guess I zoned out there for a second."

Pam lowered her voice so the others wouldn't hear. "If by spaced out, you mean you were objectifying Tammy with your male gaze, then I agree." She grinned to show she was joking. Owen looked even more embarrassed now. He glanced at Tammy again.

"She *is* pretty," he said.

"And she carries handcuffs," Joel pointed out.

Pam laughed. "Sounds like a match made in heaven."

"Made somewhere," Joel said. "Maybe you should –" He broke off, frowning.

"Do you guys hear that?" he said, shouting to be heard over the sound of the boat.

No one said anything for a few seconds, but then they all heard it: loud, high-pitched screaming.

"Gun it, Sergio!" Tammy said. "Something's happening around the bend!"

Elysium's canals curved and twisted throughout the island, and because of this, it was difficult to see very far ahead. But Sergio did as Tammy asked. He pushed the throttle forward, and the runabout picked up speed and surged toward the bend.

Tammy held onto the seatback to steady herself, and everyone else grabbed onto whatever was close by. Except Owen. He continued standing, his knees bent slightly, still recording as he swayed with the boat's motion. Owen loved shooting guerilla style, the more difficult and dangerous the job, the better.

As they swung around the bend, what Joel saw hit him like a gut punch. A girl stood on the bank screaming, while another girl – this one covered in blood – sat between two bodies. Two *headless* bodies, and she was slapping their neck stumps with her hands.

"What the actual *fuck?*" he said.

Normally, Pam swatted him on the arm whenever he cursed while Owen was recording, but this time, she was too caught up in the grisly scene before them to notice he'd said a naughty word.

Sergio throttled back hard, and the runabout lurched as it began to slow. Andrew stood up to get a better look, and a second later, Lara did the same. Joel couldn't see their faces, but he could guess what their expressions were. Andrew's would be one of detached interest while Lara would be grimacing, horrified by what she was seeing. It wasn't that Andrew was heartless. But with him, everything took a back seat to his obsession.

Pam had turned pale, and Joel thought she was fighting to keep from throwing up. Owen kept recording, and Joel knew from experience that as long as the man had a camera to serve as a buffer between him and the real world, he'd be okay.

As for Joel, he was ashamed to find himself feeling two equally strong but conflicting emotions. He was horrified by the carnage, but he was excited, too, for it meant that one of the pliosaurs had been here and might still be in the area. Maybe he wasn't that different from Andrew after all.

Sergio brought the runabout up to the bank less than ten yards from where the headless bodies lay. Tammy was the first to jump off, and once her feet hit the ground, she started running toward the blood-covered woman. Owen followed close behind, not pausing in his recording as he disembarked. After that, Joel and Pam got off, and then Andrew and Lara. Sergio remained behind to toss out the runabout's anchor before joining them on the shore.

Tammy headed for the bloody woman, who continued to smack her hands against the bodies' neck wounds.

Oh God, Joel thought. *She's trying to put their blood back.*

There was so much blood on the young woman that he couldn't tell if she was physically injured, but from the way she was moving, she didn't appear to be. Tammy obviously intended to make sure, though, but when she was less than ten feet from the woman, a lizard-like head twice the size of a horse's burst from the water. The creature moved so swiftly that Joel wasn't completely certain, but there seemed to be something wrong with the thing's mouth. Its lower jaw looked twisted out of true. But the deformation didn't stop the pliosaur from latching onto the woman's right arm and pulling her into the water.

Tammy stopped and stared at the ripples on the water's surface which were all that remained to mark where the young woman had disappeared. Then she shouldered her rifle and began firing into the water.

Andrew shouted, "No!" and started toward her, but Lara grabbed hold of his arm and held him back.

Tammy continued firing, and Owen moved around her to get a better angle. Tammy fired until her weapon was empty, and Joel gazed at the water, half-expecting a dead pliosaur to bob to the surface, but it didn't. Tammy continued dry-firing the rifle, her body shaking, and she didn't stop until Sergio walked up to her and gently took the weapon from her hands.

The other young woman was screaming even louder now, and both Pam and Lara hurried over to comfort her as best they could.

Joel stepped to Andrew's side.

"It won't be back for a while." Andrew spoke in an awed voice, as if he was having trouble making himself believe what he'd seen. "The heads were just a snack, but the girl should keep his belly full. For the time being."

Joel wanted to remind Andrew that they had just watched a person die, a person who right now was having the flesh stripped from her bones and devoured. But he said nothing. Partly because he didn't want to spoil the moment when Andrew had finally gotten to see the object of his life's quest, but mostly because he doubted his words would have any impact on the man.

Andrew turned to him and actually smiled.

"Want to join me in examining the bite marks on the bodies?" he asked.

It would make a great scene for Owen to record, Joel working alongside the infamous Andrew Rivera right after their first encounter – however brief – with a living pliosaur. But he couldn't make himself do it.

"You go ahead. I want to, uh, check with Owen and see how the recording's going."

"Suit yourself," Andrew said amiably enough and started walking toward the bodies.

As Joel watched him go, his emotions decidedly mixed, he felt a single drop of rain strike the back of his neck.

* * * * *

Brokejaw laid contentedly in the mud and silt at the canal bottom as he worked on his meal. He liked eating these things. Not only did they taste good, their hides were soft and easy to penetrate. It made it much simpler to get the meat off. Not that there was a lot of meat on this one. Not much more than had been contained in the two heads he'd swallowed earlier, actually.

He had followed One-Eye's blood trail to where one of the canals opened to the ocean. But he'd paused when he reached that point, his instincts sounded a warning. The nestlings weren't the only ones hungry after their long journey to the Beginning Place. The Matriarch and Sire needed to replenish themselves as well, and given their great size, they needed to eat much more than the nestlings. Because of this, they would attack anything in the vicinity – including the nestlings. They were driven by instinct, as were all their kind, and right now their instinct said to feed.

Normally, nestlings kept their distance from their Elders during such times, but One-Eye had chosen to return to the open water near where the Matriarch and Sire currently swam. Brokejaw didn't wonder why One-Eye had done such a foolhardy thing. He didn't remember attacking his brother earlier, but if he had, and if his small brain had been capable of reasoning, he might have come to the conclusion that One-Eye had gone to where the Matriarch and Sire were in order to keep him from following. But Brokejaw was aware of none of this. He only knew he needed to stay away from the Matriarch and the Sire for the time being, and the canals were the perfect hiding place since they were too small for the Elders to swim comfortably, and because of this, they would not enter them.

So Brokejaw had turned around and swam back through the canals, feeding on what fish he encountered – not many – and continuing to search for more of the soft-skins to eat. Hunting with his brother might be more efficient, but hunting solo had its benefits. He didn't have to share his kill, and he didn't have to go where One-Eye led. It made for a pleasant change.

He'd returned to this place because he had a vague memory of feeding here before, and he'd hoped to find food here again. He had been successful, and in hardly any time at all, Brokejaw finished his latest meal. But despite what Andrew had guessed, he was just as hungry now as he'd been before.

He started toward the surface.

CHAPTER SIXTEEN

"Tell me what you're thinking right now," Shayne said.

He was sitting in the front seat of a runabout next to Tomas, who was piloting the craft. They were the only two aboard, and this suited Shayne just fine. It allowed him to pump Tomas for information without having anyone interrupt. Although he kind of wished Lara and Pam had come with them. They were both pretty hot, especially Lara. He supposed he really shouldn't be thinking about women right now. After all, Echo *had* been dead only a couple days. Then again, he'd always been the kind of person who preferred to look forward instead of backward.

Tomas didn't take his eyes off the water as he answered.

"I don't know what you mean."

"I mean as the head of resort security, what's going through your head as you're working to …" He searched for the right phrase, scanning through his memories of the hundreds of action movies he'd seen. "Contain the situation?"

Tomas snorted a laugh.

Figures, Shayne thought. *First time I get a laugh out of Stoneface, and I wasn't trying to make a joke.*

"Right now, I'm concentrating on the task at hand," Tomas said. "Which is reaching the West Shore and finding the exact place that Echo Amato died."

"Sure, sure, I get it. Single-minded focus, job-at-hand kind of thing, right? But there has to be more than that going on in that shaved noggin of yours."

"I'm keeping an eye out for those dev–" He broke off and corrected himself. "*Pliosaurs.* Not only in case one decides to attack us, but because we need to get a better sense of how many of the damn things we're dealing with."

Shayne caught the way Tomas had started to say the word *devils* and then bailed on it. There was a story there, he was sure of it, and he made a mental note to ask Tomas about it later.

"Do you think there are a lot of these things around?"

Shayne tried not to sound nervous at the thought. An action hero wouldn't be afraid of a bunch of alligators with flippers instead of feet. The more there were for such a man to kill, the more he'd like it. But he wasn't a hero, and he couldn't completely conceal his worry.

"Not at this juncture," Tomas said. "I believe there would've been many more attacks if there were a sizable population of *pliosaurs* in the area."

At this juncture. Shayne thought that sounded so cool. He took out his phone and wrote it down using the notepad app. He hoped Tomas would use more badass phrases like that.

As they traveled, the touristy part of Elysium gave way to the more upscale surroundings. Nicer architecture, more expensive shops and restaurants, nightclubs featuring B-list entertainers, with the occasional A-lister thrown in. And then they entered the West Shore. It was like an entirely different world here, a *better* world, and although Shayne wasn't born to riches, had grown up lower middle-class, as a matter of fact, he found himself relaxing now that he was among multimillion-dollar houses with private beaches. This was the kind of place where he belonged now.

"Do you have any other weapons besides your gun?" Shayne asked.

"No. I wasn't expecting the resort to become a war zone."

"Is that what it is?" Shayne asked.

Tomas remained silent for a couple moments before answering.

"Yeah, I think so."

Tomas' reply was a simple one, but it chilled Shayne more than anything else the man had said so far. Shayne might be treating the pliosaur attacks as a career opportunity – as a game, he supposed – but Tomas was deadly serious about them.

Shayne realized where they were then, and he pointed to the bank ahead of them.

"This is it."

"Port or starboard?" Tomas asked. When Shayne looked at him quizzically, Tomas sighed and said, "Left side or right side?"

"Left," Shayne answered, embarrassed but trying to hide it.

Tomas reduced the craft's speed and pulled up to the left bank where Shayne had indicated. He killed the engine then got up from his seat and moved aft, intending to drop the anchor. But before he could do so, something large and heavy thumped against the boat's hull, nearly knocking him off his feet. Shayne was still seated, but he put his hands on the runabout's dash to brace himself. He was experiencing a most unheroic burst of panic, and it took all his control – honed by thousands of hours performing in front of live audiences and cameras – to keep himself from shrieking like a little girl.

Tomas turned back around as if deciding to make sure Shayne was okay, and then there was a second thump. The first had come from the middle of the runabout's starboard side, but this one came from the port bow. It was so hard that Shayne's ass lifted off the seat for a second, and this time, Tomas did go down, although only on one knee. The impact must've hurt like a bitch, though, because the man grimaced in pain and took in a hissing breath.

"Fuck!" he spat.

The runabout moved toward the middle of the canal, the bow spinning around so that the craft turned in a slow circle.

Shayne remembered Andrew saying at the meeting that the pliosaurs might be territorial. It sure as shit looked like the man's theory was correct.

Shayne half-turned to look over the back of his seat as Tomas stood.

"It's them, isn't?" He didn't care if he sounded like a chickenshit now. It had been one thing – a *terrible* thing – to watch these monsters kill Echo from the safety of land. But it was quite another to be on the goddam water with them.

Tomas didn't answer. Instead, he drew his Beretta and cast his gaze upon the water.

"You know how to pilot a boat?" he asked.

"Are you kidding?" Shayne said. "I'm rich. I have more boats than I have cars, and I have a shitload of cars."

"Then start it up and get us moving."

"Roger that."

Pleased at how he'd responded to Tomas' command despite his fear, Shayne hit the ignition, and when the engine came to life, he jammed the throttle forward. The runabout jerked as it started moving, but Tomas grabbed hold of the back of Shayne's seat to keep himself from falling again.

Oh my God, Shayne thought, excitement overriding much of his panic. *I'm going to be in a chase!* How lucky could a comedian who wanted to rebrand himself as an action hero get?

But before the boat could move more than a few yards, one of the pliosaurs – because really, what else could it be? – rammed into the bow again, causing the runabout to swerve toward the right bank. Shayne quickly corrected course, but then the pliosaur, or a different one, hit the bow on the other side, causing the craft to swerve the other direction. And then the two pliosaurs – it had it be two, at least – began rapidly alternating strikes, one hitting the bow on the port side, one hitting it on the starboard, over and over. The runabout rocked from side to side, and Shayne had a difficult time keeping the craft on a straight heading.

Tomas lurched from one side of the boat to the other, firing into the water. Shayne had no idea if he could see the pliosaurs, let alone if he hit them, but neither broke off their attack, so even if they had been wounded, it didn't slow them down.

"Shit, shit, shit, *shit!*" Shayne said as he fought to keep the runabout under control.

Echo's voice whispered through his mind then.

You're a motherfucking star, baby. You got this.

"I hope you're right," he muttered, as the pliosaurs continued their assault.

* * * * *

Andrew Rivera might think of these creatures as mere animals, but Tomas knew better. Could animals conceive of such a coordinated attack, one designed to prevent the runabout from escaping them and which kept the craft's occupants off balance? The devils might not be as intelligent as humans, but they were smart, and more to the point, they were *evil.*

Given the way the craft was rocking, Tomas was unable to get a decent shot at the monsters. And as big and strong as the things were, Tomas believed there was a good chance they might be able to overturn the runabout, especially if they continued attacking in unison like this. Their only chance was to put some distance between them and the devils.

"Get us out of here!" Tomas shouted to Shayne.

"What the fuck do you think I'm trying to do? Set a world record for how many times a man can shit his pants on one boat ride?"

"*Idiota*," Tomas muttered. If he got out of this alive, he would give Ysmin hell for sending him out with this blackmailing bastard.

The pliosaurs continued alternating their attacks. *Thump, thump. Thump, thump.*

Enough of this shit.

Tomas staggered aft and tossed the anchor into the water. He then shouted back over his shoulder. "Cut the engine!"

For a moment, he didn't think Shayne had heard him – or maybe was too scared to comply – but then the runabout's motor fell silent.

Tomas made his way back toward the bow, one hand on the railing. The devils struck the hull two more times and then stopped. Tomas felt grim satisfaction. He'd hoped that if they stopped trying to get away, the pliosaurs would back off. They'd been trying to prevent their prey from escaping, and now that they'd succeeded, they'd turn their efforts toward catching that prey. Tomas hoped he'd bought enough breathing room so he could get some good shots at the devils.

"Watch the port – I mean, the *left* side of the boat. Call out if you see them."

Without waiting for Shayne to reply, Tomas took up a position on the starboard side of the craft and raised his Beretta to firing position. It was at this moment that he felt the first drop of rain on his forearm. It was followed by more, until a light rain was coming down. Sudden showers were normal on *Las Dagas*. They popped up quickly and often didn't last long. Tomas was so used to them that he barely registered the rain. It was too mild to be of any concern, and besides, he had bigger problems to worry about right now.

He scanned the water, looking for any sign of the devils. At first, he saw nothing, but then he spotted a flash of white, and he remembered what Shayne had said about the pliosaurs that had attacked Echo Amato. One of them had been all white. Tomas smiled. It was quite kind of the devil to make itself such an easy target.

The white pliosaur headed toward the hull, perhaps intending to ram the boat once more. The creature was several feet underwater, but Tomas didn't think he was going to get a better shot. He aimed and started firing. He knew the water distorted the light, making it difficult to judge the devil's exact position, but the damn thing was large enough that if he aimed for the center of its mass, he felt confident he'd hit it.

He'd fired two shots when Shayne yelled, "There's one over here!"

Tomas had no idea if the Beretta's rounds had struck the white pliosaur, and now another of the devils was attacking from the port side. He cursed himself for not issuing a gun to the comedian, despite the man's pleas that he do so. Even if the bastard couldn't shoot worth a damn, at least he'd have some way of helping defend them.

He fired another round at the white pliosaur, then turned and ran to the port side. He pointed his Beretta at the water and searched for the second pliosaur.

Shayne pointed. "There!"

Tomas looked where the man indicated, and he saw a dark shape below the surface heading toward the runabout. Not as clear a target as the other one, but if everything was easy in life, where would the challenge be?

He started firing, and as before, he had no way of knowing if any of his bullets struck their target. His abuela seemed to speak to him then.

These aren't natural creatures, Tomasito. They are things of pure evil. You can't kill such things with bullets.

For an instant, he was no longer a grown man, no longer a former marine with years of training and combat experience.

Right then, he was a little boy who believed every word that came out of his abuela's mouth. At the same time, he was also a teenager who'd gazed into the soulless triangular black pupils of the evil she spoke of. He froze, rainwater streaming down his face, unable to make himself squeeze the Beretta's trigger once more. And that's when the pliosaurs struck the runabout, one hitting fore, one hitting aft. The double impact shook the craft and spun it. Tomas and Shayne grabbed for handholds, but each missed, and they both went over the side and into the water.

CHAPTER SEVENTEEN

It had started raining, lightly at first, but it was coming down harder now. Not a storm by any means, just a good soaking rain. Enough to wash away the blood on and around the two headless bodies, Pam thought. She hoped Owen had gotten good pictures of them before the rain started. The bodies would still have plenty of visual impact without blood, but *with?* No comparison.

The girl – Jenn – sat cross-legged on the grass, her face buried in her hands as she sobbed. Pam and Laura knelt next to her, Lara holding one of Jenn's hands, Pam with a hand on her shoulder. Pam saw Owen was recording Lara and her comforting the hysterical girl – or at least trying to – and while part of her wanted to tell him to give Jenn her privacy, the part of her that was a producer – and this was by far the larger and stronger of the two – was gratified. Ordinarily, she didn't like being in the video. It detracted from the illusion that Joel was a lone adventurer exploring the shadowy corners of a mysterious world. But in this case, she didn't mind. The scene was simply too good to pass up: the grief-stricken survivor of an attack by creatures that supposedly went extinct millions of years ago. She wondered if they could get Jenn to calm down enough to say a few words on camera, maybe even describe the attack. She glanced down and saw a phone lying on the ground next to the girl. Had she been taking pictures when the first attack occurred or – please, God – even video?

If so, and she could get hold of it …

You're a real piece of shit, Pam, you know that? This poor girl just saw three of her friends die!

Yes, and that was an honest-to-Christ tragedy. But she still had a show to produce, one that was going to make fucking history.

Andrew crouched next to the bodies, examining the neck stumps, and Owen had walked over to record them. Joel hung back, watching Andrew and Owen, but making no move to join them. Pam wasn't sure what was going on with him. She didn't think she was doing Jenn any good, wasn't sure the girl was even aware of their presence. So she removed her hand from Jenn's shoulder and stood. She exchanged a look with Lara, and the woman nodded to let her know it was all right if she left.

The rain had intensified, and the slope down to the canal was slippery. Pam went slow so she wouldn't lose her footing and fall on her ass as she made her way to the water's edge. She intended to join Owen and give the cameraman some direction. She doubted Andrew would take any direction from her, but if she could get him talking science, she thought he would –

The water exploded ten feet from where Owen, Andrew, and the bodies were, and the pliosaur with the deformed by all-too-functional jaw sailed through the air and landed on the bank.

Pam stopped and stared at the creature. It lay on the grass, its entire body out of the water, no more than five yards from where she stood, snout pointed toward her, as if it had been intending to attack her specifically. She was grateful she hadn't been closer to the water. Otherwise –

The pliosaur pushed with its flippers – the front set first, then the back – and it continued repeating the motion. At first, the creature didn't move, but then it began to inch forward, its smooth underbelly sliding on the wet grass. Sliding toward *her*. The pliosaur quickly picked up speed, and Pam had an absurd thought: *The fucker is surfing on the goddamn grass.*

Back at the Crescent, when Andrew had said pliosaurs were cousins to modern-day sea turtles, she'd had a hard time imagining it. But now that she saw how the pliosaur used its flippers to propel itself across the wet grass, she could believe it. Hell, it even looked like the fucker had some sort of thick-scaled armor on its back, suggestive of a primitive shell.

"Run!" Joel shouted.

That struck Pam as an excellent idea. She started to turn, intending to run farther up the bank where, she hoped, the rising slope would make it impossible for the pliosaur to follow. But she moved too quickly, too awkwardly, and her right ankle twisted. Her leg buckled and her foot slipped on the wet grass. She went down, rolled over, and faced the pliosaur as it came toward her, crooked jaw dropping to display its sharp white teeth.

The pliosaur was less than five feet from her when she heard the crack of a rifle. Tammy had taken the weapon back from Sergio, reloaded it, and now she was advancing toward the pliosaur, firing round after round. Several bullets struck the tougher hide on the pliosaur's back, but others hit the softer flesh on the sides, near the belly, and Pam was elated to see blood spurt from these wounds.

Go, Tammy, go!

More hits, more blood, but the pliosaur didn't slow down, didn't even react to being hurt. Maybe its nervous system was too primitive for the pain to register right away. Or maybe its instinct to feed was overriding everything else. Whichever the case, the pliosaur gave one last mighty push, and its teeth fastened around Pam's midsection. She had time for a final thought – *I hope to hell Owen is recording this* – and then the pliosaur bit down hard. She tried to scream, but all that came out of her mouth was a fountain of dark blood.

* * * * *

Joel watched in stunned horror as the pliosaur turned, dragging Pam along with it as it attempted to return to the water. Pam's arms and legs flopped lifelessly as the creature moved, but Joel told himself that she might have only passed out from the pain, that she could still be alive. But deep down, he didn't believe it.

The pliosaur picked up speed as it pushed itself along with its flippers, but Tammy continued walking toward the animal, firing round after round into the beast. Joel wasn't certain how many rounds a rifle held. Ten? Fifteen? The creature was bleeding from a dozen wounds now, and its pace slowed. It continued trying to push itself toward the water – which now lay less than five feet away – but its flippers could barely move. It stopped two feet from the water, Pam still clamped tight in its mouth. Its flippers quivered one last time and then stilled. The pliosaur might be dying, but it wasn't dead yet. Joel could see it still breathed, although shallowly.

Tammy lowered her rifle and continued toward the pliosaur until she was standing next to its head. She regarded it for a moment, then shouldered her rifle and placed the barrel a half inch away from the creature's left eye.

Owen started forward, as if he intended on recording the pliosaur's demise up close, but when he drew near Pam's body, saw her mouth and chin smeared with blood, her eyes open and staring, he lowered his camera and turned away. Joel couldn't tell because of the rain, but he thought the man was crying.

Andrew – who'd crouched motionless next to the boys' corpses during the entire attack –rose to his feet.

"No, don't!" he shouted.

But his words were drowned out by the sound of the rifle discharging one final time.

* * * * *

Tomas broke the water's surface and drew in a gasp of air. The rain was coming down harder now, and the air was filled with the *sssssshhhhhhh* sound of water hitting water. Normally, Tomas liked rain. One of his favorite things to do was sit at one of the tables outside the Crescent, the umbrella keeping him mostly dry, and sip a fresh cup of coffee as he listened to the sound of falling rain. But now the rain only made it more difficult to see and hear, giving the sea devils yet one more advantage. As if they needed it.

He'd lost his grip on the Beretta when he went overboard, and the only weapon he had left was a taser, and he doubted it would do more than irritate the monsters. Plus, if they were close enough for him to use it on them, he'd already be dead. There were a couple emergency flares in the roundabout which he might be able to use as weapons – *if* he could get back into the boat before the monsters attacked. The momentum caused by the pliosaurs' strikes had made the craft drift, but the anchor was keeping it from going too far, and the runabout wasn't more than a half dozen yards away. He started swimming toward it, knowing that any second he might feel sharp teeth penetrating his flesh, but also knowing that reaching the boat was the only chance they had at survival.

"Help! Help me!"

It was Shayne.

Fuck. In the confusion, Tomas had momentarily forgotten him. He was tempted to keep swimming and let the asshole fend for himself. But he was Elysium's head of security, and it was his job to protect the people on the island – all of them, not just the ones he liked. Knowing that Ysmin would kill him for doing this, assuming the devils didn't get him first, he turned away from the boat and started swimming the direction Shayne's voice had come from.

* * * * *

Shayne might not have been as strong a swimmer as Echo had been, but he spent a lot of time relaxing in his Olympic-sized pool, and he could swim well enough. So when he fell into the drink, he'd only panicked a few seconds – during which he managed to swallow a belly full of saltwater – before heading for the surface. Once his head was above water, he looked around frantically, trying to spot the pliosaurs, but he saw no sign of them.

Of course you don't, fucktard, he thought. *The bastard things are* under *the water.*

He'd been scared many times before in his life. When he'd gotten drunk at seventeen and totaled his dad's car, for example. He'd gotten banged up pretty good, and he'd thought for a while that he might die. Until he'd sobered up, anyway. And how about that time in college when he'd thought he'd gotten his girlfriend pregnant? What was her name again? Chloe? Alyssa? Turned out his goddamn roommate had put the bun in *that* particular oven. The first time he'd stepped onto a stage in a shitty comedy club in Philly to do stand-up. The first time he'd heard a movie director say *Action!* on a set. The time Rafala Wray – his co-star in a crappy movie about a horny zombie called *Stiff One* – had OD'd on heroin in the Los Angeles hotel room where they'd been partying.

And, of course, when Echo had died.

But if you took all those times and added in every other moment in his life when he'd felt fear of any sort, from a minor worry to piss-your-pants terror, it still wouldn't have equaled what he felt now. He was in the monsters' environment, absolutely helpless, nothing but prey. He couldn't make himself swim for shore, fearing that he'd only draw their attention by doing so, but he couldn't just keep treading water and wait for the fucking things to start biting off pieces of him, either. He was paralyzed, unable to act. Then he remembered Tomas, someone who most definitely was *not* helpless, and he called out to him.

"Help! Help me!"

A moment later, he heard splashing over the hiss of rain, and he thought one of the pliosaurs were coming toward him. But then he saw it was Tomas, and he was so happy he vowed to the write the man a check for a million dollars later, and maybe offer to give him a blowjob as a bonus.

A long-forgotten memory surfaced then, of him being a young boy sitting in front of the TV in his parents' living room and watching a cheesy movie on cable called *River of Blood*. In it, mutated leeches the size of sharks were rampaging up and down the Mississippi, sucking the blood out of anyone they could get hold of. At one point in the movie, the hero – a handsome-in-a-craggy-faced-way county sheriff – jumped into the river to save his ex-wife who'd fallen into the water after a mass of leeches fastened onto her fishing boat, crushing it to pieces. What was happening now was just like that scene, except they were dealing with turtlesaurs instead of leeches, and he wasn't a bleach-blonde with gigantic fake breasts. In the movie, the sheriff managed to reach his ex and helped her get to shore before the monster leeches could latch on to either of them. Shayne prayed to whatever god looked after hack comedians that this would end up being a remake of that scene.

And that's when the pliosaurs broke the surface.

* * * * *

Tomas first became aware of the pliosaurs as twin movements glimpsed out of the corner of each eye. They came at him from both sides, swimming at speeds that he wouldn't have believed creatures of their size capable of obtaining. He instinctively knew the beasts' plan: they would converge upon him, one grabbing hold of his upper body, the other the lower, and then they would tear him in two. He had no weapon to fight with, and he knew there was no way he could outrun them. There was only one thing he could do, but he had to time it just right.

He kept looking from one creature to the other, turning his head swiftly back and forth. The devils were close to the surface, and their armored backs cut through the water, almost like the dorsal fins of sharks. He couldn't see their heads, but he could imagine their mouths open in anticipation of the meat that would soon fill their stomachs, could picture two sets of reptilian eyes filled with darkness cold as the depths of space.

At the last instant before the pliosaurs – one white as bone, the other a mottled greenish-gray – reached him, Tomas took a deep breath and dove underwater. He swam downward, arms and legs moving with all the strength he possessed. He had no idea how far down he'd gone when he felt as much as heard the two pliosaurs collide. As fast as they'd been moving, they hadn't had enough time to veer off and miss each other. He knew it was too much to hope that the devils had smashed each other's skulls in, but with any luck, they'd gotten a hard enough knock to rattle their brains and slow them down.

He swam toward the surface at an angle to get as far away from the pliosaurs as he could before sticking his head out of the water to take a breath. As he breached the surface and gulped air, he couldn't keep from looking back over his shoulder. He saw water splashing and spraying as the two monsters fought, heads darting forward, jaws snapping the air as they struggled to sink their teeth into each other. Tomas felt a sense of elation. The pliosaurs' minds were too small for them to realize their prey had pulled a trick on them. All they knew was that one of their own kind had rammed into them, and they'd instinctively responded as if they'd been attacked. Hopefully, the damn things would keep fighting until they killed one another.

He knew now that the stories his abuela had told about sea devils had been nothing but superstitious fantasies. These creatures weren't evil spirits manifested in flesh. They were exactly what Dr. Rivera had called them – animals. Nothing more, nothing less. And dumb ones at that.

He turned toward the bank and saw Shayne getting out of the water. The man had obviously taken advantage of the pliosaurs' confusion to swim to shore. Shayne had probably saved his life by calling out a warning when the pliosaurs had come at him. Shayne might be a blackmailing asshole, but Tomas figured he owed the man a drink.

He started swimming for the bank.

* * * * *

The instant that Whiteback and Nub slammed into each other, all thoughts of catching their prey fled their minds. In fact, they didn't even remember there ever *had* been any prey. All they knew was that another of their kind was trying to kill them, and they responded by trying to kill the attacker first. They no longer recognized themselves as nestmates. The other was a threat that needed to be eliminated, pure and simple.

They fought close to the surface so they had ready access to air, and hissing sounds issued from their throats as they lashed out with their teeth, trying to catch hold of the other and inflict as much damage as possible. They missed far more often than they hit, and when they did manage to get their teeth on one another, they raked the hide, creating long furrows that bled profusely. But these were surface wounds only, far from fatal. They continued fighting, each searching for an opening so they could fasten their teeth on the soft flesh on the underside of the other's neck and clamp down tight, severing major arteries and preventing their opponent from being able to draw in breath. The end would come swiftly after that, and the surviving sister would feast on the corpse of her sibling.

But then, as if a switch had been thrown somewhere in their reptilian brains, they broke apart and ceased fighting. Maybe the scent of their mingled blood in the water reminded them they were nestmates. Or maybe, both being gravid with eggs, they gave off a pheromone that told them not to harm another mother-to-be. Or maybe they were simply too evenly matched and saw no point in fighting any longer. Whatever the reason, their fury drained away, as if they had never felt it in the first place. Once again, they were hunting partners, and they turned and surged through the water toward their no longer forgotten prey.

* * * * *

Tomas heard Shayne shouting. Hell, the man was practically *screaming*. He couldn't make out what Shayne was saying, wasn't sure the man was forming distinct words. But he got the message nevertheless. The pliosaurs had stopped fighting and were coming for him.

He knew he wouldn't reach the bank in time, but he refused to give up. He was a *marine*, goddamn it, and marines didn't quit. He gritted his teeth and poured every last bit of energy he had into swimming. He thought of Ysmin, of how much he was going to miss her. The only thing he truly regretted about dying was how much his death was going to hurt her. He also thought of his abuela's stories one more time, and he knew he'd been a fool to doubt them.

And then Whiteback caught hold of his left leg, Nub closed her teeth on his right arm, and the sisters pulled as hard as they could.

* * * * *

Shayne watched helplessly as the pliosaurs reached Tomas. He wanted to look away, but he couldn't move, couldn't even close his eyes. Tomas had almost made it to shore, was only ten feet or so from land, and Shayne had an excellent view of the carnage. Hell, he had a fucking front row seat.

He saw the creatures take off Tomas' arm and leg, saw blood gush from the wounds, saw the agony in Tomas' eyes. But the man didn't cry out, didn't even open his mouth. Shayne didn't know if it was because of the sudden shock of having a pair of limbs ripped away or if it was because Tomas was too much of a badass motherfucker to give his killers the satisfaction of hearing him voice his pain. Shayne wanted to believe it was the latter.

The pliosaurs gulped down their grisly prizes and then went back for more. With terrible, swift precision, they reduced Tomas' body to nothing more than a few scrapes of flesh bobbing on the water, too small for the creatures to bother with.

Shayne stood rooted to the spot, less than five feet from the water's edge. He'd paid no attention to the rain falling on him as he watched Tomas die, and he was no more aware of it when the rain began to ease up. He stared at the water, waiting for one or both of the pliosaurs to burst forth, leap out onto the bank, catch hold of him, and drag him back into the water and eat him for dessert. But the water remained calm, the only thing visible was the abandoned runabout anchored in the middle of the canal. He stood like that for five minutes before he realized the pliosaurs weren't going to return, and then he heard Echo's voice in his mind.

Poor bastard. He died and there was no one to record it. Oh well. At least he can't upstage me now, right?

Shayne turned away from the water and shotgunned the contents of his stomach onto the grass.

CHAPTER EIGHTEEN

After Tammy killed the pliosaur with the malformed jaw, Ysmin arranged for members of Elysium's maintenance staff to bring a tow truck and a flatbed to collect the creature's body. While they were working, Tammy called for paramedics to come take care of Jenn. Joel had been surprised that the island even *had* paramedics, but Tammy explained that while security took care of Elysium's policing needs, the resort had a fire station with emergency responders, along with a small hospital staffed with doctors and nurses. Such services were vital given how many people visited and worked on *Las Dagas*. The paramedics took Jenn to the hospital, and as traumatized as she'd been, Joel hoped the docs would give her some really good drugs.

Additional security officers arrived at the scene of the attacks, and they took Pam's body – along with those of the headless boys – to the hospital's morgue. Once the dead pliosaur was on the flatbed, it was hauled to one of the garages where the resort's maintenance vehicles were stored. The vehicles had been removed to make room for the pliosaur, and the creature was lowered onto a large sheet of plastic that had been placed on the concrete floor beneath bright fluorescent lights. After that, Andrew and Lara when to work immediately, examining the pliosaur and talking in excited voices as Lara used a tablet computer to take picture and make notes.

Tammy remained with the group to protect Lexana's "interest" in the pliosaur, as if the board of directors feared Joel and the others would try to steal the creature's corpse and sneak it off the island. Shayne was present as well. After Tomas had been killed, Shayne started walking back in the direction of the Crescent when a security officer driving in an electric cart found him and gave him a ride.

Now Joel stood near the pliosaur as Owen recorded him.

"What you are looking at is a creature from the dawn of time that somehow survived to ... to ..."

Joel trailed off. He couldn't remember what he'd been going to say, and he gestured for Owen to stop recording.

Owen lowered his camera.

"Don't worry about it, man. It's okay."

Joel had wanted to try recording some narration as a way of honoring Pam. He might've created *The Hidden World*, but she'd put everything she had into making the show the best it could be, and he knew she would've wanted Owen and him to keep going. This was the biggest story of their careers, hell, one of the biggest stories *ever*. She wouldn't have wanted them to miss this once-in-a-lifetime opportunity. But Joel didn't think he could bring himself to do any on-camera work. The discovery of a pliosaur species that was still alive, even the confirmation that he really had seen a pliosaur when he was a kid, meant nothing compared to the loss of Pam's life. And she hadn't been the only one to die. The pliosaurs had taken Tomas' life as well.

Pam's death had hit Owen just as hard as it had Joel, but the man was never more comfortable than when he was viewing the world through the lens of a camera. So when he moved off to record Andrew and Lara as they examined the pliosaur's body, Joel understood that it was just his way of coping.

Joel was having a hard time reading Shayne. If he was upset after having witnessed Tomas being torn apart by pliosaurs, he didn't show it. He'd said little since arriving at the garage, and now he hovered on the periphery of the examination, watching closely, brow furrowed as if he was concentrating fiercely. Maybe like Owen, the man was throwing himself into his work – in his case, conducting research for future acting roles – to cope with the trauma he'd experienced. But Shayne's eyes shone with a strange intensity that Joel found unsettling, and he didn't think the man was coping as well as he wanted the rest of them to believe.

What Joel really wanted to do was get the fuck out of here, find the nearest bar, and drink until he passed out. Instead, he walked over to the dead pliosaur to join Andrew and Lara. Now that he could see the creature up close – and it wasn't trying to eat any of them – it looked less like a nightmare made flesh and more like what Andrew kept insisting it was: an animal. It was a letdown in a way. A couple years ago, he'd dated a woman who considered herself an animal rights activist, although during their time together Joel had never seen her actually *do* anything to help animals. She wasn't even a vegetarian. Her favorite food was beef, the bloodier the better. Joel had been talking about an upcoming episode of his show, one focusing on the infamous Mothman, when she'd made a point he'd never considered before.

If things like that are real – Bigfoot, the Loch Ness Monster – I hope we never find them. Because once we catch them, they'll just end up animals caged in a zoo. Where's the wonder in that?

He hadn't been able to answer her then, and they'd stopped seeing each other soon afterward. But looking at the dead pliosaur now, he recalled her words and couldn't help feeling she'd been right.

The pliosaur's smell was strong. It hadn't had enough time to begin rotting yet, so Joel knew what he smelled was the creature's natural scent; a combination of saltwater and a thick, rank odor reminiscent of garden mulch. Other than the wounds created by Tammy's rifle, the body was mostly intact. The neck had been stretched some from where the two truck operators had fastened a leather strap in order to pull it onto the flatbed. He was surprised at how much it looked like the illustrations he'd seen over the years. Paleontologists had revised their theories about dinosaurs a number of times over the last few decades, and the current thinking was that dinosaurs had been far more birdlike than previously believed, even to the point of being covered with primitive feather-like structures. But then pliosaurs weren't dinosaurs, were they? They were reptiles, so no feathers for them.

Andrew knelt in front of the creature, examining its misaligned jaws, Lara standing at his side.

"I'm certain this isn't a congenital defect," Andrew said. "There's significant scarring on both sides of the mouth, but especially on the left side." He motioned to Lara. "Get a picture."

She used the tablet's camera app to capture an image of the pliosaur's crooked mouth.

"What do you think happened?" she asked. "Did it try to prey on something big and strong enough to fight back?"

"Perhaps," Andrew said. "Although I'm not sure what sort of creature lives in the ocean that could give our friend here that much trouble." He grew thoughtful for a moment. "Unless there are other unknown species like this that we haven't discovered yet. But if I had to guess, I'd say the injury was most likely sustained in battle with one of its own kind, perhaps even a sibling."

"I didn't know turtles were violent," Tammy said.

Andrew looked up at her and scowled, the expression on his face saying, *Who let you in here?*

"Pliosaurs *aren't* turtles," he said. "They have an ancient ancestor in common with turtles. There's a difference. And yes, turtles do fight, in their way."

"What do they do?" Owen asked. "Use ninja swords like in the cartoons?"

Owen didn't smile after his attempt at humor, lame as it was. Joel knew the man wasn't really trying to make anyone laugh. He was just running his mouth to keep his mind off what had happened to Pam. Still, he noticed Tammy did smile at Owen's joke.

Andrew didn't dignify Owen's question with an answer. Instead, he stood and took a step back, as if to admire the creature.

"Seventeen feet long, probably weighs around five thousand pounds, give or take. The thick-scaled epidermis on the back and top of the head is especially interesting. Similar protection to that provided by a turtle's shell. The creature is remarkably similar to fossilized remains that have been discovered, but based on this specimen, I'd say its species continued to evolve over time. Its body looks sleeker, more hydrodynamic, which could allow it to reach greater speeds than its ancestors. And its flippers are larger and thicker, probably to provide greater maneuverability and control while swimming at great speed."

"They'd also be helpful for maneuvering on land," Lara said, "at least in a limited fashion."

"True. It's a damn shame Lexana won't permit us to do any dissection," Andrew said, an edge of frustration in his voice. "It would be fascinating to see what the specimen's stomach contents are."

Joel couldn't believe what he was hearing.

"I'll tell you what's inside this fucking thing's stomach. Jenn's friends."

Andrew's cheeks colored. "Yes, of course. Forgive me."

Joel looked at him a moment before reluctantly nodding.

Shayne had been quiet up to this point, but now he spoke.

"Aren't you going to put this thing on ice? It's going to start rotting sooner rather than later, especially in this climate."

"We're working on it," Tammy said. "There are plenty of restaurants and hotel kitchens with big freezers on the island, but none of them are large enough to hold this thing – assuming we could find a way get it inside the building in the first place. So Ms. Strauss has ordered us to build one in here."

Owen frowned. "How are you going to manage that? It's not like that sort of equipment is just lying around."

"We keep replacement central air units in storage," Tammy said, "and we'll cannibalize metal equipment sheds and use the sections to create walls and a ceiling around the pliosaur. It won't be fancy, but it should do the job until better equipment is brought in."

"I'm impressed," Andrew said. "I suggest sealing the enclosure in thick plastic to help keep the cold air in."

"And cover the pliosaur in ice as well," Lara added.

Tammy nodded, but Joel didn't know if that meant she'd do as the Riveras suggested or was merely humoring them. Probably the former, given how important this specimen was to the Lexana Corporation.

"Until then," Andrew said, "I'll keep working." He turned to Lara. "Help me take bite radius measurements, would you?"

Lara didn't reply right away. She stared at the pliosaur's mouth, which was partially open – Joel didn't think it could close all the way given how fucked up the lower jaw was – and a number of the creature's teeth were visible. Shreds of meat were stuck between some of those teeth, meat that up until recently had been part of living human bodies.

Lara swayed and lost her grip on the tablet. The device hit the concrete floor with a clatter, and Joel feared Lara was going to follow it down. He quickly stepped to her side and took hold of her elbow to steady her.

She turned to look at him, frowning slightly, as if she didn't understand what he was doing. But then her gaze cleared and she gently pulled away from him.

"Thanks," she said, giving him a small smile to show she meant it. "I'm alright now."

Then without looking at her father, she turned and headed for the garage's exit, leaving the tablet – and all the valuable information recorded on it – where it fell.

Andrew gave Joel a questioning look.

"You dumbass," Joel said. "Did you forget how your wife died?"

A shocked expression came over Andrew's face, as if Joel had kicked him in the stomach. Joel felt no satisfaction upon seeing Andrew's reaction to his words. He was too concerned for Lara. By this point, she'd already stepped outside, so he turned and followed after her.

* * * * *

Ysmin hung up her desk phone with a trembling hand, then sat back in her chair.

The board had offered to find someone else to inform the relatives of their loved ones' deaths, but she had insisted on doing it. It was the sort of task that Tomas would've done, and attending to it personally made her feel that she was honoring his memory in some small way. Not that it had been easy, far from it. Especially this last call, which she'd made to Tomas' sister in Miami. She'd never met Luciana, nor any of Tomas' nieces and nephews, and now she never would. She couldn't even attend Tomas' funeral since nothing remained of him to bury. In a way, it was almost as if he hadn't died but vanished, quit his job and left the island without saying a word to anyone. She was having a difficult time accepting that he was dead. She kept imagining him striding into her office – a place where they had made love many times – and saying, with a wry smile on his face, *You won't believe how I got out of that one.* Tomas had seemed larger than life, so it was only fitting that he'd had an epic death. After all, how many people were eaten by a fucking sea monster?

The sound that came out of her mouth was half laugh, half sob. She pulled a full bottle of vodka from her bottom desk drawer, removed the cap, tossed it on the floor, and took a long drink. The alcohol burned all the way down her throat, and as she began to cry, she took a second drink, larger than the first.

CHAPTER NINETEEN

Lara stood outside the garage in the bright sun, relieved to be away from the pliosaur's stink. A breeze was blowing, one that was a bit too cool for comfort, and she folded her arms across her chest to shield her body. She wished she smoked. This would be the perfect time to light up a cigarette and inhale the smoke, hold it in her lungs for several seconds, and then exhale. It would give her something to occupy herself, a mindless ritual she could lose herself in, at least for the time it took the cigarette to burn to ash.

The garage was located a half mile from the Crescent, and it faced the rear of a strip mall that contained upscale shops and quaint cafes. She could see the tops of palm trees on the other side of the building, but from here, the view was primarily blank walls, back doors, central air units, and dumpsters. The view suited her mood. Elysium might seem like a paradise on the surface, but it was only a front. In a way, it was like the ocean. A beautiful surface concealing a much harsher reality beneath.

Ysmin had ordered security guards be posted outside the garage, and two men and one woman – all armed with handguns – stood near the garage entrance. Four electric carts were parked nearby. Lara and her companions had used two of the carts to get here; no way they'd wanted to take a runabout after the pliosaur attack. She assumed the guards had used the remaining carts. Lara moved away from the garage to put some distance between herself and the guards. She didn't want company right now, even if they were silent and expressionless.

She hadn't known Tomas long, and she hadn't known Jenn's friends at all. But she did know what it was like to lose someone you love, and – although she still couldn't access the memory fully – to lose that person to a monster that shouldn't exist but did.

Her mother had died in the belly of a pliosaur, one much larger than the specimen now housed in the garage. Her body lay inside the creature as its stomach acids ate away at her, reducing her bit by bit until only her skeleton remained to either be vomited up or shat out. Had her mother been swallowed whole? If the pliosaur had been big enough, it was possible. If so, how long had she survived in the monster's gut? Long enough to feel acid beginning to consume her, long enough to attempt to scream in the darkness?

"Are you okay?"

She jumped when Joel spoke, and she spun around to face him, hands half raised as if preparing to fend off an attack. But when she realized it was him, she lowered her hands.

"Sorry," he said. "I didn't mean to startle you."

"It's okay. I think we're all jumpy right now."

Except Dad. But she didn't want to say this in front of Joel. He and her father were not on the best of terms to say the least, and she didn't want to make things between them worse than they already were. Although considering how pissed off she was at her father right now, she didn't know why she cared.

"It's a hell of a thing, huh?" Joel asked.

"What is? The pliosaur?'

"Yeah, but more than that. It's weird to have a dream come true, only to realize that the reality is different than you'd imagined."

"Not different from what *I* imagined," she said.

He winced. "Sorry."

"Don't be. I understand what you meant. How are you doing? About Pam?"

He let out a long sigh.

"She was my producer right from the beginning. We did five seasons together, and she traveled everywhere that Owen and I did. That's a lot of hours on the road and in the air. We got to know each other pretty well."

Lara wondered if Joel and Pam had been in a relationship. Not that she was jealous, and it certainly wasn't any of her business, but if they *had* been lovers – and she couldn't think of a way to ask that wouldn't seem insensitive – she couldn't imagine the pain he must be feeling. But Joel answered this question for her, as if he'd sensed what she'd been thinking.

"She was family to me, like the sister I never had."

She knew that Joel had an older brother named Johnny, a physics professor in Boston who didn't approve of Joel's involvement with what he considered pseudoscience. She could relate. By assisting her father with his work, she'd sacrificed all credibility as far as the world of science was concerned. That might well change now that a specimen of a modern-day pliosaur had been obtained. But she didn't care about her father's professional redemption right now, nor did she care about hers. It meant nothing compared to the lives the pliosaurs had taken. And how many more people might die before the situation on *Las Dagas* was stabilized?

She did her best to put the thought out of her mind. "So what's next for you?"

"I don't know. Pam would've wanted Owen and me to continue working. She'd encourage us to play up her death – *Hidden World* producer killed by prehistoric sea monster! But I don't know if I have it in me to keep going. I haven't even contacted the network to let them know Pam's dead, and I haven't worked up the courage to call her family. How can I tell them the truth? They'll probably think I'm making some kind of sick joke."

"Maybe it'll be easier once the full truth about the pliosaurs is revealed," she said.

"I don't think anything will make it easier."

She couldn't think of anything to say to that, so she remained silent. She was struck by how Joel was reacting to Pam's death, as well as the deaths of Jenn's friends. The Joel Tucker she'd known wouldn't have hesitated to use those deaths to their fullest dramatic effect in his show, all in the cause of furthering his quest for the truth. She knew *The Hidden World* was primarily a means to an end for Joel, and that nothing mattered more to him than finding proof that cryptids did indeed exist. She supposed his single-mindedness – which wasn't so different from her father's – had been one of the things about him that had attracted her in the first place. But when he'd wanted to exploit her mother's death on his show, he'd gone too far. She'd found his willingness – more, his *eagerness* – to use someone else's tragedy and pain for his own ends to be revolting.

But he was different now. Less self-centered, more empathetic. She liked him much better this way. Too bad her father would probably never develop those traits. Some beings evolved and some didn't. She knew which kind Andrew Rivera was.

"I'm ready to go back inside," she said, then smiled. "Thanks for coming to check on me."

He returned the smile, nodded, and they went back into the garage.

* * * * *

When Andrew saw his daughter enter the garage with Joel, his first thought was, *Christ, not again!* When Joel had first contacted him several years ago to ask if he could feature Andrew and his research on *The Hidden World*, Andrew had agreed, but only because of Joel's enthusiasm for the subject and his knowledge of Andrew's work. Andrew hadn't known anything about the show, so he watched a couple episodes and was appalled at how awful they were. One episode had featured an urban legend about an evil scientist named Dr. Crow and mutant children that he'd created called Melonheads. Andrew had thought Joel had made up the ludicrous story until he'd checked online and found it to be an actual – if no less ridiculous – bit of modern folklore.

He'd been tempted to contact Joel and cancel the interview, but Lara had talked him out of it. She said maybe he could bring a more rational, scientific viewpoint to the show. And if his appearance on the program boosted his book sales, so much the better. They could use the money. After all, it wasn't as if they had any university grants or corporate sponsorship to fund their research. So Andrew had decided to go through with it. They arranged to meet in Santa Monica, and once Joel and his crew arrived, Andrew was surprised to find them pleasant and professional. He was even more surprised to see that Lara was attracted to Joel right away and vice versa. As the old saying went, sparks flew between them, and since Lara had sacrificed having a life of her own to assist him, he didn't object when she and Joel began dating. After a few weeks, he thought the relationship might develop into something serious, and he wasn't sure how he felt about that. But then Joel did something – Lara refused to tell him what exactly – and she broke it off with him. She'd been angry and hurt and, although he wasn't sure she admitted it to herself, disappointed.

For causing Lara so much pain, Andrew had put Joel at the very tippy-top of his shit list, and the man had remained there ever since. He had not been happy to learn that Joel had come to *Las Dagas* for the same reason he and Lara had, but since there was nothing he could do about it, he'd decided to ignore Joel as much as possible. But seeing him walk in with Lara like this made him decide to change his strategy. Instead of ignoring Joel, he would keep a close eye on him, and if it looked like he was going to make a play for Lara again … well, parents had to look out for their children, didn't they? It was one of the most fundamental laws of nature.

Owen was standing next to Tammy, as were Andrew and Shayne, and the cameraman turned to Joel and Lara as they entered.

"You won't believe what Tammy's been telling us."

Joel and Lara joined them, and Tammy repeated her story.

"When the canals were being constructed, workers came across a cave near the ocean on the north side of the island. Inside, they found paintings on the walls, like the stuff that cave people draw, you know? I heard about the place when I first started working here, and I thought it sounded cool, so I decided to check it out. It took me a while to find it, but eventually I did, and it was just like I had heard. The cave, the paintings, everything."

Andrew could tell by the blank expressions on Lara and Joel's faces that they didn't understand the relevance of Tammy's story.

"Tell them what the paintings depict," he said.

Tammy pointed to the dead pliosaur.

"Really?" Lara said.

Tammy nodded, grinning.

"I've asked her to take us there," Andrew said, "and she agreed."

"That's fantastic!" Joel said.

Andrew scowled. When he'd said *us*, he'd meant Lara and himself. But he supposed he couldn't stop Joel and Owen from coming, so he saw no point in trying.

"We can leave right now if you're done here," Tammy said. "To tell the truth, I'll be happy to get out of this place. That damn thing smells like something that spilled out of a backed-up sewer."

Andrew could spend weeks examining the pliosaur's remains, but seeing Tammy's cave was too good an opportunity to pass up.

"I'm coming, too," Shayne said. When no one said anything, he added, a trifle defensively, "Ysmin will insist on it."

The others exchanged glances and then gave a metaphorical group shrug. Whatever.

They headed outside to the electric carts. On the way here, Tammy had driven one cart, and Andrew, Lara, Joel, and Owen had all squeezed in, barely managing to fit. With the addition of Shayne this time, they were going to have to take two carts.

"I'll drive one," Tammy said. She looked at Joel. "Do you mind driving the other?"

"Sure," he said.

Owen chose to ride with Joel, as did Shayne. Andrew and Lara got in Tammy's cart.

Before either Tammy or Joel could press the cart's ignition, Andrew said, "Damn it! In all the excitement, I left the computer tablet lying on the floor. I'll be right back."

He climbed out of the cart quickly before Lara could offer to go get it for him, and he hurried back into the garage, not looking at the faces of the guards. Once inside, he closed the door behind him and walked up to the dead pliosaur. He stood directly in front of the creature's head, gazing down on it. He paid no attention to the tablet computer lying on the concrete floor several feet away. Tammy hadn't turned off the garage's fluorescents when they'd left, and the bright light illuminated every detail of the pliosaur, right down to each line and crack in its mottled hide. Andrew regarded this ancient creature, this miracle, for several seconds before unzipping his shorts, pulling out his cock, and releasing a stream of hot urine onto the pliosaur's head. He kept going until his bladder was empty, then he gave his dick a couple shakes before tucking it back in and zipping up his pants once more. As bad as this fucker smelled, he doubted if anyone would realize someone had pissed on it, but if they did notice, he didn't give a shit.

Everyone, including Lara, thought his research was all about proving that pliosaurs as a species still lived. But they were wrong. One of these monsters had killed his wife, and that was something he could never forget – or forgive.

Lara called him Ahab sometimes, when she wanted to complain about how obsessed he was with finding proof of pliosaurs' existence. She'd been more right than she'd known. Like Ahab, all he cared about was getting revenge, but in his case, it was on the whole fucking species of pliosaurs. He wanted to learn everything he could about them – how they lived, where they lived, how they traveled ... wanted to know their strengths and, more importantly, their weaknesses. Because once he knew enough about the bastards, then he could tell the rest of the world how to go about killing them. It wouldn't be hard to convince the world that the pliosaurs were monsters that needed to be wiped out. They'd killed enough people on the island, and the uploaded videos of the attacks had already primed people to view the pliosaurs as vicious and dangerous.

"Your kind should have died out ages ago," Andrew said to the pliosaur's piss-wet head. "But you didn't. That's a mistake I intend to rectify."

He hocked up a wad of phlegm and spat it onto the pliosaur's head for good measure, then he retrieved the tablet and headed for the exit to join the others.

CHAPTER TWENTY

One-Eye was *hungry.*

He'd had little to eat since being attacked by his brother yesterday. The injury to his right rear flipper – caused by the late Tomas – was healing, but it still slowed him down, enough that prey too often escaped his teeth. Not that there was much prey to be had right now. There should've been many fish in the water around the island, far more than what he could find in the canals. But the hunting was poor because he wasn't the only predator here, and he wasn't the only one whose belly cried out to be filled. The Matriarch and the Sire had traveled just as far as the nestlings, and they needed to restore their energy reserves, too. This was the reason the waters around *Las Dagas* were so bereft of prey. The Matriarch and Sire had been circling the island, eating constantly, and the prey that was fortunate enough to escape them had fled into the Great Deep.

One-Eye's instincts were at war. He wanted to avoid another confrontation with Brokejaw – or one with Whiteback and Nub – until he was back to full strength, and for this to happen, he needed to feed. But he also wanted to stay as far away as possible from the Matriarch and the Sire. They wouldn't hesitate to devour him if he came too close. Pliosaur pods functioned as effective hunting and breeding cooperatives, but family bonds didn't exist between their kind. When the hunger was upon them, all that mattered was eating, and any meat would do.

So far One-Eye had managed to keep his distance from the elder pliosaurs, but his hunger had grown so strong that it was beginning to override his other instincts, and he wasn't paying as much attention to his surroundings as he should have. He needed meat, and he needed it *now*.

A dark, shadowy thing – a structure of some sort on the ocean floor – caught his attention, and he swam toward it. A quarter mile off the island's north shore, a sunken ship rested on the bottom, and had for fifteen years. The *Rosa del Mar*, a fishing trawler out of Nicaragua, had gotten caught in the outer edge of a hurricane because the captain – a barely functional alcoholic named Ernesto Martinez – thought he could evade the worst of the storm and get a few more hours of fishing in to try and make up for what had been an especially poor season that year. Ernesto's foolish pride had cost him and his crew their lives when the *Rosa del Mar* went down, and the wreck became their communal grave.

The ship was discovered during the first six months of Elysium's operation, and it had since become a popular attraction for divers. None were here today, though. No one was suicidal enough to risk diving after the pliosaur attacks, which was unfortunate for One-Eye. He would've loved to tear into one of the soft-skins right now, but he'd take what he could get. Fish liked to hide in such places, he knew, and he hoped to find some there.

He glided toward the corroded remains of the *Rosa del Mar*. The ship had come to rest at an angle, listing starboard, and was half buried in mud and silt. The bodies of Ernesto and his crew had been reduced to skeletons by marine life long ago, and there was no scent of rotting meat in the water to entice One-Eye. He circled the wreck slowly, senses alert for any potential prey – small fish, octopi, sharks – which might be using the wreck to hide from the Matriarch and Sire. He detected no sign of life on his first revolution around the ship, but he continued circling. If he were lucky, his presence might alarm something enough to spur it into making a move, after which he would race toward it and – hopefully – feed at last.

He was halfway through his third revolution when he felt the water around him quiver slightly, and his instincts screamed a warning. He darted to the side just as the Sire came rushing toward him, mouth open wide, teeth bared. The Sire missed One-Eye by less than three feet, and the swift passage of his great bulk sent a wave rushing toward One-Eye, pushing him forward and causing him to lose his balance. In his desperation to feed, the Sire had misjudged his strike, and he slammed into the *Rosa del*

Mar. The vessel was sixty feet long, roughly thirty feet larger than the Sire, but the sea had been working on the ship for a decade and a half, weakening its structure. So when the Sire struck the wreck, it broke apart beneath the elder pliosaur's weight like it was made of rotted wood. Mud and silt rose like a cloud around the Sire, momentarily concealing him.

One-Eye was scarcely aware of all this. He was too busy trying to regain control in the now turbulent water. If his flipper hadn't been injured, he could've performed this task with ease, but now it was a challenge. And if he couldn't manage it, the Sire would soon be after him again. His collision with the *Rosa del Mar* might have stunned him for the moment, might have cut and scraped his skin, but there was little likelihood that he'd been seriously injured. One-Eye needed to get away from here *now*. He gave a final push with his three fully functional flippers, and he shot forward a dozen feet, reaching slightly calmer water. If he had been human, he would've felt a surge of triumph mixed with relief. But the only thing he felt was his instincts shouting for him to get moving, The Sire was twice his size, and given his current disability, there was no way One-Eye could outrun him unless he had a really good head start.

But before he could begin swimming in earnest, he felt the water quiver again, more strongly this time, and once more his instincts sounded a warning. One-Eye shot upward as the Matriarch came at him from the side, but he wasn't fast enough this time, and the tip of her snout struck him on the back, just above the base of his spine. His protective back armor was thinnest there, and the impact caused it to crack. Fiery pain lanced up his spine and pierced his brain like a harpoon. He spun nose over tail as the Matriarch rushed past beneath him, and he splayed out his flippers – even the injured one – in order to halt his spin.

It took several seconds before his body was once more completely under his control, and by this time, the Matriarch had slowed and was beginning to turn back toward him. To make matters worse, the Sire had regained his wits and emerged from the silt cloud and was now headed this way. It would be a race to see which of them would reach him first, but whichever caught him, he knew he would end up in the Matriarch's belly, for the

Sire would turn him over to her if he reached One-Eye before her. The Matriarch always ate first.

One-Eye saw only one chance, and he took it. He swam toward the Sire, and at the last instant before the Sire could clamp his jaws down on the nestling, One-Eye veered right and continued on, swimming as fast as he could toward the cloud of silt that surrounded the broken remnants of the *Rosa del Mar*. If he could reach the cloud before the Elders could reach him – and before it dissipated too much – he might survive this.

As he raced toward the cloud, he sensed both the Matriarch and the Sire orienting on him. Given their much greater size, they were slow to turn, but once they got going in a straight line, their speed was incredible. One-Eye forced himself to swim even faster. His spine still throbbed from the blow he'd taken, and his injured flipper was a white-hot ball of agony. But he didn't allow his pace to slacken. His life quite literally depended on speed now.

He managed to reach the cloud before the Elders could catch him, and once he was completely concealed, he shot off at a downward angle and headed straight for the sea floor. He plowed into the mud and silt, rolling as he did so to cover his body with black muck that would not only camouflage him but, with luck, would also mask his scent. He wriggled into the mud until he was half buried, and then he closed his eyes and grew still. He didn't hope, and he certainly didn't pray. He simply lay there, hiding as best he could, and whatever would happen next would happen. That's what life was in the end: one gamble after another, and too many of them longshots.

He sensed the Matriarch and the Sire swimming above him, crisscrossing the area as they searched for the tasty nestling that was proving more difficult to catch than they had expected. The search seemed to continue for a very long time, and soon One-Eye's lungs were crying for air. He had expended a great deal of oxygen evading the elder pliosaurs, and he needed to return to the surface and replenish his supply of air. If the Matriarch and Sire didn't leave soon, he'd be forced to abandon his hiding place and make a dash for the surface. And if he did, in all likelihood he'd be dead before he could reach the halfway point.

But then he sensed emptiness in the water above him, as if the Elders had departed. Maybe it was true, or maybe it was only his species' version of wishful thinking, but he couldn't remain submerged any longer. He pushed himself off the bottom and swam toward the surface with as much speed as his injured and exhausted body could muster. He expected to feel large teeth sink into his flesh any second, but it didn't happen, and then his head broke the surface and he could breathe. He remained floating on the surface for several minutes, resting as he continued to draw in the sweet air. He knew he made an easy target floating motionless like this, but he was too weak to care.

After a bit, he felt vibrations in the water and he became instantly alert, anticipating another attack. But then he saw an object in the distance, one of the things his kind sometimes encountered during their journeys across the planet's oceans. He had no concept of *ship*, but he did know that these objects only moved across the water's surface, and that they carried the soft-skins.

After working so hard to avoid becoming a meal for the elder pliosaurs, One-Eye – who had been hungry before – was now *ravenous*. He was tempted to start swimming toward the ship in the hope of snagging a soft-skin or two. But he knew the chances of that were slim. Better to return to the island where he'd had success in feeding before. And as far as his siblings, he'd have to do his best to avoid them. He had to feed, and that meant he had to take a risk. Another gamble in a lifelong series of them.

He started swimming toward the island.

* * * * *

The Sire was nervous. The nestling had escaped both him *and* the Matriarch, and she was furious. The hunting in the island's vicinity was not as good as it had been when they were here last, over a decade ago. He had no way of knowing, let alone understanding, that the presence of humans on the island – with their fishing and increased water traffic – had been the cause for the decline in the sea life population. All he knew was that if the

Matriarch didn't feed, and soon, she would turn to the nearest available food source – which would be him.

He felt it then, the same vibrations that One-Eye had sensed, and he also knew what they meant: *food*. The Matriarch and he would follow these vibrations, and unlike the nestling, they were large enough to do something about them.

In no way did he communicate his intention to the Matriarch. He didn't have to. When he turned in the direction of the vibrations and started swimming, she turned and followed without hesitation. It was the Sire's job to find them food, and so where he went, she followed. He hoped this hunt proved more successful than the last, for if it didn't, the Sire would fulfill his task as provider of meat one final time.

* * * * *

What would Tomas do?

Shayne had been asking himself this question since they'd left the garage. He hadn't made a conscious decision to try to think like the man, but it was as if his subconscious had decided that by doing so he'd be keeping the man alive. He told himself that he was only working toward the goal that was his reason for joining the investigation: preparing himself to step into the role of an action hero. It *wasn't* because he felt guilty for blackmailing Ysmin into letting him tag along with the others, or because Tomas would most likely still be alive if he hadn't had to babysit Shayne when those two pliosaurs attacked the runabout. No, no. It was all about the research, nothing more.

So as the pair of electric carts and their passengers drove through the streets of Elysium at a speed not much faster than Shayne could jog, he sat up straighter and squared his shoulders, affecting what he hoped looked like a military bearing. He then tried to see the world through Tomas' eyes. He supposed the man would've been driving one of the carts – too late for that now – but he'd been head of resort security, right? So even though they were driving toward a cave to see some old paintings, Tomas wouldn't be thinking about that. He'd be keeping an eye out for any sort of trouble, ready to jump out of the cart and bust some heads together if it became necessary. He'd be *suspicious*, of everyone one and everything. He'd trust no one except himself, not completely. Everyone was a potential suspect in a crime that hadn't been revealed yet.

He'd scowled a lot, Shayne recalled, so he furrowed his brow. And Tomas' lips were usually pressed together in a tight, disapproving line. Shayne did this as well. Tomas would be aware of the gun riding on his hip, and he'd be ready to draw it and start firing at the first sign of trouble. They had no weapons in their cart, but Tammy had her rifle with her in the other one. Andrew and Lara rode in the back seat, and the rifle lay with its butt on the cart's floor, its barrel leaning against the passenger side of the front seat, in easy reach should Tammy need it.

Shayne needed a gun. Not a rifle, though. A handgun like Tomas had carried. He wondered if he could get hold of one here on the island. He'd probably have to steal a gun from a security officer. He should probably see about getting a uniform to wear, too. When it came to researching a role, he believed it was important to strive for *authenticity*. Then again, if a rifle was all he could get his hands on, he supposed he could make it work.

In his mind, Echo laughed with approval.

First rule of show business, she said. *Learn to be flexible.*

Shayne smiled. Oh, he could be flexible. He could flex like a motherfucker when he had to.

As they continued heading toward the north side of the island, where Tammy said the cave was located, Shayne decided it would be best if he started to refer to himself as Tomas, but only in his mind. He knew the others wouldn't understand. After all, they weren't artists like him.

So he amended his earlier question. Not what would Tomas do? But –

"What would *I* do?" he whispered.

* * * * *

The road ended at the edge of a beach, so they parked the carts, disembarked, and started walking. Tammy led the way, rifle in hand, and the rest followed. Andrew and Lara behind her, then Joel and Owen – who was recording video, naturally – and then Shayne, bringing up the rear. Joel was surprised by that. Shayne was a movie star, and out of all of them, he should want to be in the camera's frame at all times.

The jagged rocks that gave *Las Dagas* its name – the daggers – were prominent here, a cluster of them rising from the water a few hundred yards off shore. Seventy feet tall and black as obsidian, they were a sinister presence, like the teeth of some unfathomably giant monster that had been buried beneath the earth for eons and was now rising to break its million-year-long fast. Thanks to the pliosaurs, Joel knew he would never look at those rocks the same way again.

When they were halfway across the beach, Joel glanced back over his shoulder at Shayne, and the man smiled.

"Don't worry. I've got our six."

Joel didn't have any idea what he was talking about, but he nodded anyway and then faced forward once again.

The sky had become overcast, the clouds thicker, darker, and more numerous than they had been when it rained earlier. *Looks like we're in for a real storm this time,* he thought. He hoped it would hold off until they were done checking out the cave.

A strong breeze blew in off the ocean, but the temperature had dropped since they'd set out for this side of the island. The wind made him shiver, and he wished he was wearing a pair of thick jeans instead of thin shorts. The waves breaking on the shore were loud, seeming to release jittery, pent-up energy. Normally, he loved the sound of ocean waves, but these were far from peaceful and relaxing.

The wind must be stronger out to sea, he thought. Just as he was thinking the storm might turn out to be worse than he'd first guessed, bright lightning flashed in the distance, followed a couple seconds later by a loud crack of thunder.

"That was close," he said out loud, to no one in particular.

Tammy stopped walking and motioned for them to halt. She took the handheld radio from her belt, pressed the transmit button, and began speaking.

"Dispatch, this is Officer Chu. I'm on the North Shore assisting the people investigating the animal attacks. It looks like we've got some nasty weather coming our way. What's the radar show?

"*Hey, Tammy. This is Nick. Yeah, there's a good-sized storm brewing about ten miles out to sea. But right now, the wind's blowing southeast, so I think the worst of it's probably going to miss us. We'll get more rain than we did this morning, and it'll last longer, but it shouldn't be too bad.*"

"*If* the wind doesn't change direction," Tammy said. She thanked Nick for his help and tucked the radio back onto her belt. "You heard the man. Let's keep going."

She started walking again, and after a moment's hesitation, during which everyone but Shayne cast a doubtful eye at the approaching storm, they followed once more.

Joel had a bad feeling about their little expedition, but he figured he was just being paranoid. After everything that had happened today – losing both Pam and Tomas – how much worse could things get?

CHAPTER TWENTY-ONE

The cave was easier to reach than Joel expected. He had pictured a tiny opening set halfway up a craggy cliff face, but the cave opened directly onto a stretch of sand wide enough for two people to walk shoulder to shoulder if they wished, and its mouth was wide enough for three people to pass through side by side. Four if they were skinny. The cave was part of a flat rock face that rose fifty feet above the beach. It looked to Joel like a section of the island had sheared away from the rest long ago, like a sheet of ice detaching from a melting glacier.

They stopped outside the cave and peered in. It was gloomy inside, but not pitch dark. If the sun had been out, they probably could've seen quite a way inside. It was almost depressingly non-scary, but Owen recorded video of the entrance anyway.

Joel heard music then, faint and coming from a distance. Party music with a driving beat. He and the others turned toward the ocean and saw a white catamaran a mile off shore, maybe less. It was cruising slowly, and Joel could see people on deck. They were too far away for him to make out any details about them, but from the music, he assumed they were out for fun. He had a hard time imagining wanting to go on a party cruise after people had been killed by real live sea monsters, but the deaths likely hadn't affected any of the partiers personally, and Elysium *was* a resort. People came here to enjoy themselves. Too bad it looked like the approaching storm was going to spoil their festivities. At least their craft was large enough so they wouldn't have to worry about being attacked by pliosaurs.

They turned their attention away from the catamaran and back to the cave.

"Does it have a name?" Andrew asked.

"Not that I know of," Tammy said. "*Las Dagas* had some small settlements on it at one time, but the island was used primarily as a stopover point for sailors and fishermen. If any of them ever named anything besides the island itself, there's no record of it."

She removed the flashlight from her belt and switched it on.

"Shall we?" She said this with a smile. The question was supposedly for all of them, but it was Owen she looked at.

"After you," he said, returning her smile.

Joel wanted to say, *Get a room, you two*, but he kept his mouth shut. After losing two of their number to the pliosaurs today, he didn't much feel like making jokes.

He glanced at Lara, but like her father, her attention was focused entirely on the cave. If she was still thinking about her mother's death, she seemed to be handling it well enough.

Tammy led the way into the cave, shining the flashlight before her, and the rest of them followed.

* * * * *

Wesley Mathis was *bored*, and if there was one thing he hated more than anything else in this world, it was being bored. That was why he'd moved to *Las Dagas*, bought his boat – which he'd named *Sea Be Jammin'*, and started Regal Island Yacht Cruises: to avoid boredom. And during the year he'd been in business so far, it had worked remarkably well. He took out groups of partiers every day, and he had a blast playing host. He paid other people to pilot the boat, serve as crew, and tend bar, while he worked hard to make sure his guests had a blast, drinking, dancing, and laughing along with them. Sometimes they'd stop and put down anchor so people could swim, but most of the time they cruised around the island, partying and soaking up sunshine.

He was – and he thought this completely without irony – living the dream.

Three years ago, he'd been an ENT surgeon with a thriving practice in Pittsburgh. His wife Jeannie sold real estate, and while their careers kept them too busy to have children, they felt fulfilled and, for the most part, happy. Then Jeannie found a lump in her breast, and despite early and aggressive treatment, the cancer's deadly march throughout her body couldn't be stopped, and seven months after her diagnosis, she was gone.

He tried to go on without her, but he found himself caught in the grip of an existential crisis. He was performing the same surgeries over and over, and while he was helping people – and being paid very well for it – his work began to feel like drudgery. Jeannie's death had shown him that life was too short to waste even a minute of it. He knew he wanted to stop being a surgeon, but he didn't know what he wanted to do instead. So he decided to take a vacation, get away for a while, and clear his head so he could think. And the destination he chose was Elysium. He stayed there two weeks, and when it came time to go home, he realized he didn't want to. Elysium *was* home. He returned to Pittsburgh long enough to sell his practice and his house, empty his bank accounts, buy *Sea Be Jammin'*, and then he returned to Elysium and intended to remain there, partying until the day he died. And party he did. When he wasn't hosting parties-for-pay on his boat, he was partying on the island. His life was a blur of booze, drugs, sex, and music, and he'd never been happier.

He was as surprised as anyone when prehistoric monsters showed up on the island and started eating people. But it didn't take long for him to see the business opportunity here, and he started hosting monster-spotting parties, taking out people who were eager to get a glimpse of the *Las Dagas* Monsters. He'd been running one cruise after another around the clock the last couple days, and he'd barely had any sleep. He was functioning on caffeine and self-prescribed stimulants, and he was wired and irritable. He could use the extra money, though. There was a lot of upkeep on his boat, and fuel and booze weren't free. Neither were employees. But the monster-hunters were so fucking *dull*. They barely drank anything and didn't dance. They spent most of the time at the railing, binoculars in front of their faces, scanning the water for any sign of monsters, leaving him with nothing to do but drink alone and stand around with his dick in his hand until it was time to head back to the dock.

A storm was rolling in now, though, and once it broke, with any luck he could cut the cruise short. And if he had to pay out some refunds because of it, who fucking cared? He'd just be glad it was over.

Wes stood at the bar, leaning his elbows on the counter, a bourbon on the rocks next to him, untouched. He was afraid alcohol would just make him sleepy at this point, and he didn't know why he'd ordered it. Habit, he supposed. He was in his fifties, but fit, and while his hairline was receding, he still had hair, and he dyed the gray to match his natural black. He wore classic middle-aged beach bum attire: a T-shirt with the words SUCK MY CONCH on the front, white shorts, and sandals.

"Excuse me?"

He turned to see an attractive tanned blonde in her late twenties, wearing cut-off jeans shorts and a white bikini top. He'd noticed her when she got on board, of course, but she hadn't paid him any special attention then, and she'd continued to ignore him ever since. But here she was now, looking quite tasty. Maybe this trip wouldn't be a complete waste after all.

"Can I help you?" he asked, giving her a smile that was half-friendly, half-lascivious. "That's why I'm here, after all. To tend to your needs. Every one of them."

She made a face as if he'd just farted out of his mouth.

"Would you mind turning off the music?" she asked. "Some of us are afraid it might be scaring away the monsters."

His smile became strained.

"No problem."

The woman thanked him and left, heading back to the railing to resume her search.

With a heavy sigh, Wes turned to the bartender.

"Raul? Do you mind?"

The boat's sound system controls were set into the wall behind the bar. Raul gave Wes a nod, pressed a button, and the music died. Wes felt like part of him had died as well. The music had been the only good thing about this trip. Fuck it. He didn't care how much extra cash he could pull in doing monster cruises. After this trip was over, he was going back to party cruises exclusively. Fuck these monsters.

He picked up his bourbon and drained half the glass in a single gulp. He paused, enjoying the pleasant burn of the booze, and then he drank the rest. He held out the glass – empty save for three half-melted ice cubes – to Raul.

"I'll take a double this time."

* * * * *

The Matriarch swan by the Sire's side now. She'd detected the vibrations and honed in on them, and she no longer required him to lead. As they drew nearer the surface, she saw the silhouette of what she took to be a large creature. A whale? The shape wasn't quite right, and the vibrations were all wrong. It didn't matter. She didn't care what it was as long as she could eat it.

The vibrations changed then, became less intense. This worried the Matriarch. Strong vibrations meant activity, perhaps even prey that had been wounded and was in distress, making it easier to kill. But when their vibrations lessened, it often meant that the prey was weakening, perhaps even close to death. The Matriarch didn't mind eating the dead. Meat was meat. But she enjoyed the hunt, the chase, the struggle, and the kill. Meat was all the sweeter when she had to work for it.

She increased her speed, hoping to reach the prey while some fight remained to it. The Sire was momentarily left behind, but he quickly increased his pace and soon swam even with her once more. Together, they surged toward the silhouette of *Sea Be Jammin'*.

* * * * *

"They're over here," Tammy said.

She led them deeper into the cave. The floor was wet, rocky, and uneven, and everyone stepped carefully to avoid twisting an ankle or falling. Tammy stopped in front of a particular section of cave wall and shined her beam on it. When the paintings were revealed, Joel was so stunned he actually gasped.

The renderings were crude but easily identifiable. In the middle was a brown circle surrounded by black triangles. *Las Dagas.* The island was encircled by greenish-gray pliosaurs, their snouts all pointed toward the island, as if they were swimming toward it. They were arranged in what appeared to be small groups. Two big ones and four smaller ones. Owen was of course recording, and he stepped past Joel to get a closer shot of the paintings. The colors were faded, the edges of the images blurred. Untold years of being exposed to sea air had degraded the paintings, but they were still intact enough to make out.

"How long do you think they've been here?" Joel asked.

"Impossible to say without performing tests," Andrew said. "And geology is not my field. Neither is anthropology. But if I had to guess, I'd say at least a few hundred years, perhaps longer."

"Look at the way the pliosaurs are grouped," Lara said. "Do you think whoever painted this was trying to indicate the animals travel in pods?"

"It could well be," Andrew said.

"If that's true, we have a problem," Shayne said. He spoke in a brusque, confident voice very different from his usual nervous patter. "There are at least four pliosaurs in the area. That would make them the four small ones. So where are the two bigger ones? And how *much* bigger are they?"

Everyone looked at Shayne for a moment, unsure what to make of his pronouncement or of the strange manner in which he'd made it.

"There *have* been reports of boats missing," Tammy said. "The pliosaurs we've seen so far aren't large enough to bring down a boat by themselves. Not a good-sized one, anyway."

They were all silent for a moment as they tried to imagine a pair of gigantic pliosaurs lurking in the waters around *Las Dagas*.

"There's this, too," Tammy said, swinging her flashlight beam to the left. "I figure these were added later."

The beam illuminated a series of numbers that had been carved into the rock by some kind of blade, most likely a knife.

1698, 1711, 1719, 1728.

Owen stepped closer to get a better shot of the numbers. "What are these? The sailor equivalent of 'we were here'?"

"Possibly," Andrew said, but he sounded doubtful.

"The interval isn't exact," Lara said, "but in general, there's a ten-year span between the numbers. Sometimes more, sometimes less, but that seems to be the basic pattern."

"Whoever did this made sure to carve the dates near the paintings," Joel said. "Maybe they were recording the years the pliosaurs came to the island."

"That's a good theory," Andrew said. "And if the pliosaurs only lay eggs approximately once a decade – at least only lay them *here* once a decade – it would explain why they haven't been sighted until now. Elysium was constructed in the last few years, *after* their last visit."

Andrew looked at the others for several more seconds before glancing back at the paintings. Joel wondered if he was imagining the way they'd look reproduced in the book he no doubt planned to write about the *Las Dagas* Monsters.

"There's one other thing about the paintings," Shayne said. "They don't show just one pod coming to the island. They show many."

For a moment, no one said anything as they processed this, and then Shayne – who no one knew secretly thought of himself as Tomas – gave voice to what they were all thinking.

"What if the pliosaurs that are already here arrived early? What if more are coming? A *lot* more?"

* * * * *

"Look! There's one! And it's *huge!*"

"There's another! My God, they're *gigantic!*"

Wes had finished his latest drink and was about to order a third when his passengers started shouting in delight and amazement – although more than a few sounded afraid. People who'd been standing elsewhere on the boat keeping lookout for monsters now came running to where the others stood, looking out over the water and pointing in excitement.

He hadn't really given much thought to whether or not the monsters truly existed. As long as people paid him to take them out in search of the things, it didn't matter to him if they were real or not.

Wes went over to join them and see what the fuss was about. It was raining now, and the wind had kicked up quite a bit, but he ignored the weather. He pushed his way through the crowd gathered at the railing, looked in the direction everyone was pointing, and nearly shit his pants. There were two of them, and they were indeed huge. Fifty feet long, he guessed, maybe more. They were like something out of a cheap monster movie, the kind of thing he might've watched on Saturday afternoon TV when he'd been a kid. But there was nothing fake about them. He could see the way their muscles moved beneath their skin as they swam, the way their tongues quivered eagerly inside their wide-open teeth-filled maws. But worst of all was their eyes. He could see a primitive intelligence working in them, along with a hunter's cunning and predatory hunger.

They were magnificent and terrifying in equal measure, and part of him was grateful that he'd had the opportunity to witness such wonders. For the first time in a while, he thought of Jeannie and wished she were here to share this moment with him. But a more rational part of him, the part that had gotten him through medical school and helped him have the confidence to cut up other human beings for a living, pointed out a very important detail about the monsters. They were heading straight for *Sea Be Jammin'*, and they weren't slowing down.

Shit!

He pushed his way back through the crowd and ran toward the bridge, shouting.

"Get us moving!"

But the pilot didn't hear him and he was only halfway to the bridge when the giant pliosaurs reached his boat.

CHAPTER TWENTY-TWO

Joel hadn't noticed when the party music on the catamaran stopped, but he heard people cheering and shouting off in the distance. That sound was quickly replaced with screaming, and *that* was followed by a crashing noise that he first took for more thunder. But he didn't think it was thunder.

They hurried outside to see what was happening. It had begun to rain, and it was coming down hard enough to instantly soak them. *Looks like the wind did change direction,* Joel thought. *Big-time.*

Out on the water, a pair of giant pliosaurs were attacking the catamaran. The monsters slammed their bodies against the starboard side again and again, causing the craft to rock dangerously. Joel remembered the dream he'd had during his first night on the island, in which dozens of massive pliosaurs attacked the cruise ship he'd been on as a child. In a way, this was like watching that nightmare come to life.

"There has to be something we can do!" Lara said, and without thinking, Joel stepped to her side and put an arm around her shoulder. Andrew noticed and scowled, but said nothing and returned his attention to the pliosaurs.

"I think it's too late," Joel said softly.

Lightning flashed and thunder roared as the monsters attacked. Rain and wind lashed them, but they were unaffected by the storm. The humans gathered in front of the cave entrance watched as the catamaran broke apart beneath the pliosaurs' onslaught. People fell off the deck and into the water, and the pliosaurs quickly snapped them up. The two halves of the ship began to sink, but the pliosaurs didn't intend to wait for that to happen. They leaped up onto the decks – one pliosaur per half – and tore into any passengers unfortunate enough to be in the vicinity of their jaws. The monsters' weight caused the broken halves of the catamaran to sink faster, and within moments, they had slipped beneath the waves. Joel knew that if there were any survivors left floating on the water, the mega-pliosaurs would make quick work of them. It had taken only a few minutes, but the catamaran was gone and everyone aboard was dead. And Joel and the others witnessed it all.

Joel turned to Owen. The man had captured the entire attack on video, but he was shaking hard, and Joel knew for once the camera hadn't insulated the man from what he'd seen. He lowered the camera to his side, and he was so pale, Joel thought he might throw up. He knew just how Owen felt.

"Jesus Christ," Tammy said. "That was the most horrible thing I –"

The woman got no further. A smaller pliosaur – the one they'd seen before that was missing an eye – came flying out of the water toward her, mouth wide open. The creature landed on the beach close to Tammy and fastened its teeth around her left leg. Her hands sprung open and she dropped the flashlight she'd still been carrying and – far more importantly – she dropped the rifle. Tammy screamed in agony and reached down to strike her fists on the pliosaur's head, trying to force it to release her, but her blows had no effect. Blood poured from the wounds on her leg, soaking the pliosaur's snout, only to be diluted by rainwater and washed away. The pliosaur began shoving itself backward with its flippers, intending to carry its prey back into the ocean.

Just like crocodiles pull their prey into the water to drown it, Joel thought

Owen dropped his camera and ran toward Tammy. He took up a position behind her, wrapped his arms around her waist, and pulled. She howled with pain as Owen and the one-eyed pliosaur played tug of war with her.

Joel had no idea what he could do to help, but he couldn't just stand there and watch Tammy die. He started forward, but before he could go more than a couple feet, Shayne dashed forward, snatched the rifle off the ground, shouldered it, and started firing at the pliosaur. He aimed at the lower half of the creature's neck instead of its armored back, and a series of wounds opened in the animal's flesh. The pliosaur didn't release Tammy, but it shook its head violently, as if in pain. Tammy was yanked back and forth, and her leg snapped with a sickeningly sharp sound. Owen lost his grip on Tammy when the pliosaur shook her, but he grabbed hold of her once more, his face a mask of determination. Shayne continued firing, and Joel ran forward, intending to grab hold of Owen and his add his strength to the cameraman's. But as he reached toward Owen, the pliosaur gave a mighty push backward, probably as much to escape the rifle's bullets as to pull its prey into the water. The creature slid back into the ocean, pulling Tammy along with it, and since Owen refused to let go of her, he went with them.

"No!" Joel shouted as Owen and Tammy disappeared beneath the waves.

He started toward the water, intending to run out into the surf and find Owen and Tammy, grab their hands and pull them back before … before …

Lara took hold of his arm to stop him. He tried to shrug her off, but just as Owen hadn't let go of Tammy, she wouldn't let go of him.

"They're gone, Joel," she said. "I'm sorry."

He turned to her, wanted to shout that it wasn't too late, that there was still a chance, but he knew she was right, and he remained standing where he was.

"Is that another one?" Shayne said, pointing toward the water with his free hand.

Joel, Lara, and Andrew looked in the direction Shayne had indicated. Lightning flashes illuminated the water in bursts, and they saw something out there, farther away than the one-eyed pliosaur could possibly have reached in such short time. But as Joel looked, he realized it wasn't merely one shape. There were more, maybe as many as a half dozen – no, two dozen – and they were all heading their way through the storm-tossed waves.

"The rest of them have arrived," Andrew said.

Joel thought of the paintings, of the ring of pliosaur pods pointed toward *Las Dagas*, and he pictured that happening now, hundreds, maybe thousands of pliosaurs racing toward the island to lay their eggs, all ravenously hungry after their long journey.

"We've got to get away from the water," he said. "Now!"

He grabbed Lara's hand and started running, pulling her along with him. He paused only long enough to grab Owen's camera. He didn't give damn about *The Hidden World* anymore, but he didn't want Owen's work to be lost. It was the least he could do for his friend. Andrew followed, as did Shayne-who-thought-he-was-Tomas, still carrying Tammy's rifle.

* * * * *

One-Eye was hurt, hurt *bad*.

He'd managed to drag his prey into the water, though, and what was more, he'd snagged a second soft-skin in the bargain. But he was in too much pain to kill them both right now, so when the second soft-skin let go of the first, One-Eye swam off, carrying only the one he already had in his mouth. He hated to waste the meat, but there was no help for it. He could sense others of his kind drawing near the Beginning Place, and he knew how hungry they would be. If he allowed them to get close enough to him, they would immediately sense his weakness and tear into him. But fleeing the area would only be a temporary respite. The other pliosaurs would enter the canals, just as he and the nestlings in his pod had, and sooner or later, one or more of the newcomers would catch up to him and kill him. He had only once chance for survival. He needed protection, and the only ones who might provide it were Whiteback and Nub. If he brought the meat he'd caught – which now flopped lifelessly in the current as he swam – to them as an offering, if he presented himself as the subservient male to their dominant females, they *might* protect him from the others.

It wasn't much of a chance, but it was the only one he had, so he did his best to ignore the pain of his injuries and went off in search of the nearest canal entrance.

* * * * *

When they were underwater, the pliosaur gave a yank and Tammy slid out of Owen's hands. He reached for her frantically, but it was no good. The one-eyed pliosaur had turned and was already swimming away, carrying Tammy along with it. He wanted to swim after them, wanted to do *something* to save Tammy, but he knew it was hopeless. Even the greatest human swimmer in the world couldn't hope to keep up with one of those monsters, even a wounded one.

He swam toward the surface, his heart heavy. He wasn't sure what had compelled him to try to save Tammy. He'd never done anything heroic before, had always felt more comfortable observing rather than participating. When you participated, you had to make *choices*, and Owen hated that. What if you chose wrong and made everything worse?

But when the pliosaur had fastened its teeth on Tammy's leg, he hadn't thought. He'd simply reacted. And not because he'd fantasized that Tammy and he had some kind of special connection, that they were destined to become lovers. Sure, he'd liked her and had been attracted to her, but they'd known each other less than a day. Maybe after they'd lost Pam he hadn't wanted to see anyone else die because of those fucking monsters. Or maybe he'd finally grown tired of standing by and recording while others did what needed to be done. Maybe he'd decided his time had come to get involved at last.

Not that he had done any good. Tammy was dead, her body nothing more than food now.

He reached the surface and drew in a deep breath, feeling guilty for still being alive when Pam and Tammy – and Tomas – weren't. He did his best to shove the negative emotion aside. There'd be plenty of time to wallow in guilt once he was back on shore.

It was raining harder now, and the wind had caused the waves to become larger and wilder. He rode the swells as he attempted to orient himself. The sky was almost as dark as night now, and he was having a difficult time determining in which direction shore lay. Lightning flashed nearby, followed closely by near-deafening thunder. But the momentary burst of illumination showed him land was off to his left. He'd gotten a glimpse of Joel and the others running along the beach, and he tried to cry out to let them know he was alive. But the wind was howling now, the lighting and thunder more frequent, and his voice was swallowed up by the cacophony. Fuck it. He'd catch up with them later.

He started swimming.

He hadn't been very far from shore when he'd first reached the surface, maybe a hundred feet at most. But the turbulent waves had carried him farther out to sea, and now he was a hundred-and-fifty, maybe two hundred feet from shore. He swam as hard as he could, but he felt he was doing little more than staying in place, or perhaps just floating out to sea more slowly. But he wasn't about to give up, He'd keep swimming until he reached shore or sank from exhaustion and drowned.

As it turned out, he didn't have to worry about the latter.

He didn't see the mass of pliosaurs coming up behind him. But he felt it when the first one reached him and sank its teeth into his right calf. And he felt it when the second bit into his side. After that, so many pliosaurs were on him, biting, tearing, and ripping that soon he didn't feel anything but a distant numbness, as if he were experiencing his own death from far away, once more an observer here at the end.

And then he was gone, and the pliosaurs – none of which had gotten much more than the merest taste of his meat – continued toward the island, bellies screaming to be filled.

CHAPTER TWENTY-THREE

By the time they reached the carts, the rainfall had gone from heavy to torrential, and the sky had grown so dark that Elysium's streetlights had come on. There were four of them left now – Joel, Lara, Andrew, and Shayne – and they all fit into a single cart. Not that climbing in did much to shield them from the storm. The cart did have a roof, but with the wind blowing as hard as it was, the rain more often than not came at them sideways. Still, some shelter was better than none. And while it might've been drier in the cave, no way in hell did Joel want to be trapped there with a horde of hungry pliosaurs converging on the island. He'd seen how the one with the twisted jaw had been able to surf on wet grass, and that had been during a light rain. He didn't want to imagine a dozen pliosaurs sliding across wet sand toward the cave, all fighting to get at the tasty meat hidden inside. They were all better off being cold, wet, and miserable, but *not* being eaten.

Joel put Owen's camera on the floor between the front and back seats. The device was soaked, but he wanted to keep it from being further damaged if he could. Andrew's tablet computer was back there, too. All the information and images they'd gathered about the pliosaurs, now in one place.

"We have to get hold of Ysmin," Shayne said, shouting to be heard over the shrieking wind. "We have to let her know what's coming!"

"I've got a phone," Joel said. He pulled it out of his drenched shorts, intending to call the Crescent, but the phone's screen was dark.

"It's dead," Joel shouted. He jammed the useless device back into his pocket. "Anybody else have one?"

Andrew didn't, but Lara and Shayne did, but theirs were just as waterlogged and dead as Joel's.

"It might not just be water damage," Andrew said. "The storm may have knocked out the cell towers. My ship is moored not far from here, and I have a satellite phone on board. We can use it to contact Ysmin."

Shayne, still holding onto Tammy's rifle, shook his head in vigorous denial.

"It would be faster and easier to drive to the hotel." He paused, then added, "It's what Tomas would've done."

Joel frowned. There was something odd about the way Shayne said this. The cadence of the words sounded unlike him. In fact, they sounded more like the way Tomas had spoken. And Shayne's eyes didn't look quite right, either. They were too wide and seemed almost to glitter with internal light, as if he'd taken a really strong drug of some kind, though Joel hadn't seen him take anything. Joel feared the man's mind had snapped.

"I think it's best if we stick together," Joel said. Having a crazy man with a rifle riding with you wasn't an ideal way to travel, but he didn't want to abandon Shayne, not after the way he'd stepped up and tried to save Tammy and Owen.

"Please, Shayne," Lara said. "We ... we could use your help."

Shayne trained his wide-eyed gaze on Lara and cocked his head.

"Who's Shayne?" he asked. Then he jumped out the cart, climbed into the driver's seat of the other vehicle, and set the rifle down next to him. He activated the ignition and pulled away, heading in the Crescent's direction.

"What the *fuck* was that?" Joel said.

"It doesn't matter," Andrew said. "We need to get to my ship."

Andrew had taken the driver's seat when they'd gotten into the cart. Lara sat next to him, and Joel now sat in the back alone. Andrew hit the ignition and the cart began to move. He started driving in the opposite direction than Shayne – whoever he thought he was – had taken.

* * * * *

Shayne drove as fast as he could through the streets of Elysium. The cart wasn't made for speed, and the rain and wind made it difficult to keep the vehicle under control. But he couldn't afford to go any slower. Ysmin needed him, and he'd rather die than let her down. Because he wasn't Shayne Ferreira anymore. He was Tomas Palomo, head of Elysium's security and Ysmin's lover. At least, he *thought* he and Ysmin were lovers. The way Tomas – no, *he* – had stood close to her during the meeting this morning, the glances they'd exchanged, the way the tones of their voices softened when they spoke to one another … They all indicated a relationship much closer than a merely professional one.

No, he wasn't some candy-ass actor pretending to be a hero. He was the goddamn genuine article, the kind of man who would never let his woman down, who was always there when she needed him. Not like that piece of shit Shayne, who'd only stood and watched as a monster killed *his* girlfriend, a woman more talented than he could ever hope to be.

Dark as it was, between the streetlights and the periodic flashes of lightning, he could see well enough. The cart's tires hadn't been designed to operate in extreme weather conditions, and he could feel the small vehicle hydroplane from time to time. But he steered into the direction of the swerve each time and managed to keep the cart on the road. It helped that the streets were deserted for the most part. No other vehicles were on the road, only an occasional pedestrian running to get out of the rain. If he could keep going like this, he'd reach the Crescent long before those losers made it to the old man's ship. Fucking cowards.

He heard a woman's voice.

That's right, baby! You can do it! Go, go, go!

The voice was familiar, but he couldn't put a name to it. He shrugged and put the voice out of his mind. He could worry about who it belonged to later. Right now, he had work to do.

He came to an intersection, blew past the stop sign, and hung a sharp right. For a second, the cart was running on two wheels only, but then the others came back down, and he continued on. He could tell by the railing on his left that he was paralleling one of the canals, and he wondered how much rain they could handle before flooding. A lot more than this, he decided, and even if the water level rose, the sloping banks on either side of the canals were high enough to prevent the water from flowing into the streets.

So he was confused when he saw a pliosaur in the middle of the street ahead of him, chewing on what was left of a woman – or maybe a man. Given the body's current condition, it was hard to tell. He backed off the accelerator as he drew closer to the creature, and he tried to make some sense of the damn thing's presence. He'd already established for himself that the canals wouldn't flood, so how had this motherfucker ... Then he remembered what Joel and the others had said about the pliosaur that had killed Pam. The bastard had been able to move around on land because the grass had been wet. *The damn thing actually surfed on the ground,* Joel had said. The way the rain was coming down now, it had created a layer of water for these things to slide across. And as long as it continued to rain this hard, the fuckers could climb out of the canals and pretty much go wherever they wanted. If meat wouldn't come to them, then they'd go to it.

Too bad she – or he – didn't make it inside in time, the mystery woman said.

"Yeah." Shayne stopped the cart ten feet from the feeding pliosaur, picked up the rifle, and got out.

The creature had been so involved in its meal that up to this point, it hadn't noticed Shayne's arrival. But as he started to walk toward it, wind and rain pushing against him with every step, the pliosaur pulled its blood-covered snout from within the woman's ravaged body cavity, and with a swift motion turned to look at Shayne. The rain quickly washed the blood from its snout, but it didn't do anything to remove the gobbets of flesh stuck beneath its teeth. Its eyes filled with hate, and it jutted its head forward and opened its mouth wide. Shayne thought it hissed at him, but with all the noise of the storm, he couldn't be certain. He didn't know whether the pliosaur viewed him as a potential threat, a second helping, or both. Whatever the case, it pushed with all four flippers and shot toward him, the smooth skin of its belly sliding easily over water-covered asphalt.

Shayne would've been terrified to see a monster like this coming at him, mouth open, teeth bared. But Tomas wasn't frightened. All he felt was steely calm. He raised the rifle, aimed, and fired three shots directly into the pliosaur's maw in rapid succession. The creature's head jerked back as blood sprayed from its mouth, then its head flopped to the side, and its body half rolled over as it continued sliding toward him. He stepped to the side to avoid it, but he needn't have bothered. Without the flippers to propel the body, the creature quickly lost momentum and came to a stop two feet away from where Shayne had stood.

He stepped toward the pliosaur and smacked the rifle butt against the side of the thing's head. It didn't react, and that was good enough for him. The fucker was dead. He turned his back on the corpse and started toward the cart. He climbed in and put the rifle on the seat next to him once more.

Good job, hon, the woman said.

"Thanks."

He hit the ignition and the cart started moving. He drove around both the dead pliosaur and its victim. Once past them, he floored the accelerator and continued on to the Crescent, keeping a sharp eye out for any more landsurfing pliosaurs.

* * * * *

"Go left!" Joel shouted. "*Left!*"

"I see it!" Andrew shot back.

A pliosaur was sliding down the street toward them, mouth open and ready to eat. It was the fourth one they'd seen on land so far, but it was the first that looked as if it was going to catch them. But just when it appeared they were going to collide with the monster, Andrew yanked the cart's steering wheel to the left, and they swerved barely in time to avoid it. As it was, the pliosaur snapped at Joel, and it was close enough to fling spittle onto him. As they zipped past, the pliosaur spun around with a speed and ease only made possible by the rain. It then began slapping its flippers on the ground and propelled itself after them.

Lara turned in her seat to watch the pliosaur.

"It's following us!" she shouted.

"I've got the pedal floored!" Andrew yelled. "This is as fast as it goes!"

As fast as it can carrying this much weight, Joel thought. *But if one of us were to jump off ...*

He was about to do it when they passed an ice cream shop filled with people that had crammed inside to escape the storm. The interior lights were on, giving the pliosaur an excellent view of what lay behind the establishment's front windows. The pliosaur altered course and slid toward the shop, flippers working feverishly. The people inside screamed and tried to back away from the glass, but there were too many of them and they had nowhere to go. The pliosaur crashed through the window, slid into the shop, and started biting mouthfuls of flesh from whoever was unfortunate enough to be closest. Blood sprayed the air as screams of fear became shrieks of agony. The sounds grew fainter the farther Joel, Lara, and Andrew traveled, but it was almost a minute before they could hear them no longer, even with the noise of the storm.

Lara's face was ashen, and Joel – who figured he probably looked the same – reached over the seat back, put a hand on her shoulder, and gave her what he hoped was a reassuring squeeze. She reached up and covered his hand with hers and squeezed back.

Andrew didn't appear to have any reaction at all to what had happened to those poor bastards in the ice cream shop. His brow was furrowed, his eyes squinted against the rain. He gripped the steering wheel so tight his knuckles were bone white, and the cords on his neck were so taut, they looked like they might snap any second, like guitar strings that had been tightened too much. He looked like a man possessed, and there was something about him that Joel found equally as frightening as the pliosaurs in its own way. Maybe Shayne wasn't the only one of them who'd lost it. Then again, given what they'd experienced today, he wasn't confident that any of them were completely sane at this point.

"Is the camera okay?" Andrew asked.

Owen's camera still rested on the floor of the cart between Joel's feet.

"It's still here," Joel said.

"Good," Andrew said. "I still have the tablet. Tucked it into my shorts against the small of my back. We have to protect them both. They're my proof."

"Don't you mean *our* proof?" Lara said.

Andrew gave her a look Joel couldn't interpret, but then he smiled and said, "Of course."

They continued on for another block without seeing any more pliosaurs, and then the cart began to slow.

"What's wrong?" Lara asked.

"Fuck!" Andrew swore. "I think the battery's running out of charge."

The cart continued crawling along for a dozen more feet before stopping.

"Looks like we're walking," Joel said. He scanned the area, searching for any signs of pliosaurs, but he saw none. Maybe they'd driven far enough away from the canals by now, too far for the pliosaurs to go. Yes, it was raining like a sonofabitch and the monsters could surf along the ground, but that didn't mean they felt safe venturing too far from the canals. He hoped.

"We only have a few more blocks to go," Andrew said. "But we'll have to be careful."

At first, Joel didn't know what he meant, but then it hit him, and he felt like a moron. They were going to Andrew's ship. Which was moored at a dock. On the water.

He supposed they could sit here and wait out the storm. Ysmin was probably well aware of the pliosaur invasion by now, so there wasn't any need to use Andrew's satellite phone to call her. They'd be cold and uncomfortable if they stayed here, but –

Lara was looking past him, and now she pointed without saying a word. He turned and saw a pliosaur – no, two – come sliding around the corner of the street.

"Time to go," Joel said.

The three of them climbed out of the cart and started running.

CHAPTER TWENTY- FOUR

The storm had knocked out the Crescent's electricity. Power outages during storms were, unfortunately, a normal part of island life. They were so common that sometimes it seemed to Ysmin the power would go out if someone on the island released a particularly strong fart. The hotel's back-up generators were running, but the storm showed no sign of letting up, and it was possible they would run out of fuel before the storm blew itself out. Ysmin didn't give a shit. If the lights went out again, the guests would just have to sit in the dark until morning. And if any of them tracked her down to complain, she'd tell them to fuck right off. She was in no mood to deal with anyone's bullshit, not even her own.

She sat at one of the tables outside the hotel, its large canvas umbrella only providing partial cover from the rain. She didn't mind getting wet, though, didn't care if it ruined her outfit – an expensive Italian suit jacket, blouse, and matching skirt. She wasn't wearing any shoes. She'd kicked them off before stepping outside. She'd brought the bottle of vodka with her, and it sat open on the table, a quarter emptier than it had been when she'd first sat down.

The tables – six of them – had been placed here because of the ocean view. It was one of the loveliest spots on the island, and there were always guests here, enjoying the tranquil beauty of *Las Dagas*. Tomas had loved to sit here and sip warm coffee when it rained, and she'd loved sitting with him. During those times, she'd felt like they were the only two people in the world, and she'd wished it would go on raining forever.

The rain wasn't relaxing today, though, and that was fine by her. The weather was a perfect counterpoint to how she felt right now. It was dusk, and the sky was turning even darker than it already was. Lightning still flashed every few minutes, and the thunder was so loud she could feel the tabletop vibrate and see the surface of the vodka in the bottle shiver.

She didn't know why she felt so awful, so empty, like nothing mattered now and never would again. Sure, Tomas and she had been close in a physical sense, but their relationship had been a casual one. Yes, they'd had sex almost every day, more than once a day when they could manage it, given their schedules. But they'd never spoken about their feelings for each other, and neither of them had come close to saying the L word. She supposed the best way to describe what they'd been to each other was friends with benefits. So while it was completely understandable that she should mourn the loss of a friend, why did it feel like someone had reached into her chest and tore her fucking heart out?

Just because neither of you said the L word doesn't mean you didn't feel it.

She took another swallow of vodka. Some dribbled past her lips and down her chin, but instead of wiping it away with her hand, she leaned back until her head was outside the umbrella's protection, and she let the rain wash it away for her. When she straightened, she looked toward the ocean, and that's when she saw it. Dozens of what looked for all the world like baby turtles leaving the ocean and making their way onto the beach. But that didn't make any sense. Baby sea turtles left the beach to go *into* the water, not the other way around. And from where she was sitting, she shouldn't be able to make out any details about them. The distance was too great. They should look like tiny dots from here. But she could see their heads, flippers, tails ... but no shells.

The fog of grief combined with alcohol lifted for a moment, and she understood that what she was looking at weren't tiny turtles. They were full-sized pliosaurs. A shitload of them. Lexana's board of directors might think a few pliosaurs on *Las Dagas* could be exploited for their benefit, but once the world found out the island was infested with the goddamn things, as if they were giant marine cockroaches, it would be the end of Elysium. Lexana might come out ahead it if was able to establish ownership of the pliosaurs somehow, but her job – her *life* here – would be over.

It was already over the moment one of those fuckers killed Tomas. This is just the icing on the death cake.

She grabbed the vodka bottle by the neck, stood, and started walking toward the beach.

* * * * *

Shayne was more fortunate than Joel and the others. The battery on his cart held out long enough for him to reach the Crescent. But as he pulled up to the hotel, he saw Ysmin get up from one of the outside tables, a bottle of booze in her hand, and start walking toward the ocean. An ocean that had disgorged a fucking horde of pliosaurs onto the beach. What the *hell* was she doing?

What else? came the woman's – Echo's – voice. *The director just called action, and she's started the scene. But this isn't just any scene, lover. This is the one where the hero gets to save the girl. Now get out there and give 'em hell!*

"I will," Shayne promised.

He parked the cart on the road not far from the tables, grabbed the rifle, jumped out, and started running after Ysmin. He could hear music – a driving rock tune perfect for a high-tension action scene. The lightning and thunder heightened the atmosphere, and he couldn't believe how realistic they were. The special effects department was *killing* it today. Wind tore at him, rain pelted him, and he'd never felt more alive.

"Ysmin!" he called out. "Stop! For the love of God!"

The dialogue was corny, but he felt confident that his performance could sell it.

He doubted she could hear him over the storm, so he pushed himself to run faster. He had to catch up to her before the first of the pliosaurs reached her. It was going to be close. The damn things had spotted her and were heading straight toward her, dozens of them slapping wet sand with their flippers, mouths open and eager as they advanced.

The leading edge of the pliosaur mob was only twenty feet away from Ysmin by the time Shayne reached her. He grabbed hold of her arm and she stopped, but she took a drink of vodka before looking at him. She blinked as rainwater ran down her face and into her eyes, and she leaned her head toward him, as if to see him better.

"Shayne?" she said.

Great. Her first line in this scene, and she'd blown it. He was *Tomas*, not Shayne. He thought about breaking character and starting over, but he didn't hear the director yell cut, so he decided to keep going. Hopefully, they could fix Ysmin's fuck-up in post.

He started pulling her back toward the hotel.

"Come on! We have to get out of here or those fucking things will tear into us like we're an all-you-can-eat buffet!"

Christ, who wrote this shit?

Ysmin pulled free from his grip. "Fuck off. I'm exactly where I want to be."

It looked like the crazy bitch wanted to commit suicide by pliosaur. Was that in the script? It didn't matter. Nobody was going to die today, not on his watch.

The creatures were closing in, and Shayne was tempted to throw Ysmin over his shoulder and make a run for it, but he had a better idea. He decided to go for it, and if the director didn't like it, they could always do a different take. He stepped in front of Ysmin, shouldered the rifle, and started walking toward the oncoming pliosaurs.

"Dinner's been canceled, assholes," Shayne said, then began firing.

Now that he saw the pliosaurs up close, he couldn't believe how damn scary they looked, and to achieve this kind of realism with practical effects displayed astounding craftsmanship. He wouldn't be surprised if whoever designed these bad boys got an Oscar nod next awards season.

He fired once, twice, but when he tried a third time, nothing happened. He was out of ammo.

"Goddamn it!" He lowered the rifle and looked around, trying to spot the director. "Who was supposed to make sure the fucking gun was loaded?"

There was no reply, and Shayne frowned. He saw no director, no crew, no cameras. There was only him, Ysmin, and the monsters racing toward them. For the first time since parting from Joel, Andrew, and Lara, he questioned if he was making a movie after all.

Real, not real. What's the difference? Echo said. *All that matters if you're going to die a legend. Like me.*

And then the pliosaurs were on him, and he only had time for a short scream before one of them tore his throat out.

* * * * *

Ysmin watched as Shayne went down, swarmed by ravenous pliosaurs that ripped into him like a pack of wild dogs. Funny. For a moment there, he'd reminded her of Tomas.

She raised the vodka to her lips, but before she could get a last drink, pliosaurs crashed into her, knocking her to the wet sand, and teeth began tearing at her flesh. She'd dropped the bottle, and its contents poured into the sand, mixing with rainwater and blood.

* * * * *

Feasting on the passengers and crew of *Sea Be Jammin'* had taken the edge off the Matriarch's hunger, but she was by no means satisfied.

Once she finished nosing through the wreckage on the ocean bottom, double-checking for any morsels she might have missed, she turned her attention to the Sire. He'd been swimming in slow circles above the wreckage while the Matriarch inspected it, but when she raised her head to look at him, his instincts sounded an alarm. His first impulse was to flee. She was larger than he and more massive, but this meant she was less maneuverable. If he started swimming now at his top speed, and if he could maintain that effort long enough, he had a better than even chance for survival. And then, once his instincts told him it was safe to approach her once more, he would do so, falling back into his subservient role without resentment or animosity.

But he hesitated.

155

Making sure the Matriarch was fed was his responsibility. She still hungered and there was no more food in the area – except him. The concept of self-sacrifice, even on the most basic animal level, was alien to his kind. But while his instincts were shouting at him to flee, they were at the same time urging him to remain where he was and let the Matriarch do what she must. So he continued swimming in his circle, a compromise between fleeing and staying in place.

The Matriarch rose toward him, slowly at first but with increasing speed. Her mouth yawned wide as she came, and the Sire – still swimming – tensed his body in anticipation of the pain to come.

But at the last moment, the Matriarch broke off her attack. Nestlings swam past them, hundreds of them, none belonging to their pod. The Sire understood at once what was happening. The Others had arrived.

The Matriarch snapped at any nestling that was foolish enough to swim too close to her teeth. Most proved too fast and escaped unharmed, but not all. The Matriarch was chewing on the wriggling body of one such slowpoke when the Elders came into view. They emerged from the water's gloom as large dark shadows, but as they swam closer to the Matriarch and Sire, their features became more distinct. They swam in pairs – each the Matriarch or Sire of their own pods – and the pairs kept enough difference between themselves and the others to cut down on the risk of potential conflict.

Like the Matriarch and Sire had been when they'd first arrived at *Las Dagas*, the other Elders were hungry after their long journeys from across the globe, and they were desperate to feed. But what little food had been in the area, after the soft-skins had caught it or drove it away, had gone to fill the bellies of the Matriarch and Sire. And the nestlings had all swam on and were out of reach. There *was* no food ... save for the Elders themselves.

A female almost as large as the Matriarch darted toward the Sire, fastened her jaws around his neck before he could react, and gave him a vicious shake. There was a loud *snap*, and just like that, the Sire was dead.

The Matriarch felt no sorrow upon seeing her mate die. What she saw was another female holding onto meat that was rightfully hers, meat she intended to reclaim. She surged forward, teeth bared, prepared to fight to the death.

CHAPTER TWENTY- FIVE

Joel was impressed – and profoundly relieved – that they encountered few pliosaurs during the last leg of their journey to the dock. There wasn't a beach here, but rather a stone wall erected between the land and the water, which he assumed had been created to be a wave-breaker during a storm like this one. If so, it was doing its job. Waves crashed into it, sending up spumes of foam, but the bulk of the water was held back. Since getting on shore here was difficult at best, even with surging waves to lift them higher, it seemed most of the pliosaurs had sought easier places to make landfall. This suited Joel just fine. After everything they'd been through, he figured they deserved a break. They were able to avoid the few pliosaurs they saw, and they reached Andrew's research vessel – the *Wayfarer* –without getting eaten.

Once they were aboard and out of the rain inside the main crew cabin, which also served as a galley, Andrew said, "The sat phone's in my quarters. You two go call Ysmin, and I'll check out the camera and tablet to see how badly damaged they are."

He removed the tablet from his pants and held out his other hand for the camera, but Joel was reluctant to turn it over. The device contained Owen's last work. Pam's, too. He was reticent to relinquish it, but it had been drenched by rain, and he needed to know if they could salvage the video. He handed the camera to Andrew.

"I'll take good care of it," he reassured Joel. "I'll be in my work room. Let me know if you reach Ysmin."

Andrew got a plastic bag from one of the cabin's cupboards, put both devices inside to protect them from the rain – not that it probably mattered at this point – then stepped outside.

"Come on," Lara said. She took his hand and led him back out into the rain. They moved along the deck toward the *Wayfarer*'s aft, opposite the direction Andrew had gone.

Joel hadn't been on the *Wayfarer* since he'd interviewed Andrew for *The Hidden World*, but Andrew's cabin looked exactly as it had the last time he'd seen it. A single bed – covers rumpled – a nightstand, a small dresser, and an equally small closet. Ocean maps tacked to the walls, covered with lines and notes written in red marker. Books and printouts stacked in lopsided piles on the nightstand and floor. He wondered if Andrew had touched any of it over the last couple years, or if it had all been sitting there, left to gather dust.

"Where does he keep the sat phone?" Joel asked.

"Honestly, I'm not sure." Lara glanced around the cabin. "Maybe in his dresser or closet."

Lara checked the dresser, Joel the closet, but after a couple minutes of searching, neither of them had found the phone.

And that's when they heard the *Wayfarer*'s engine start up.

The ship lurched and Joel grabbed the top of the dresser to steady himself, while Lara took hold of his arm to do the same.

"What the hell?" Joel said.

"Dad's taking the ship out. I don't know why."

The only reason Joel could think of was that Andrew wanted to go out on the ocean to try and get a closer look at the mega-pliosaurs before they swam out of the area. But while that seemed perfectly in keeping with the Andrew Rivera he'd come to know – the obsessive researcher who lived and breathed pliosaurs – it didn't scan. He sensed something else was going on with Andrew, but he hadn't the faintest idea what it could be.

"We need to get to the bridge," Lara said.

She grabbed his hand once more – he thought he could get used to her touch again very easily – and together they exited the cabin and flung themselves back into the storm. The bridge was located toward the bow from here, and they made their way across the deck, holding each other's hand tight, as wind and cold rain lashed them like whips made of ice.

Joel squinted his eyes against the rain, and he looked past the railing. The *Wayfarer* was definitely moving. Andrew had pulled it out of its slip – no doubt having cast off the lines when Joel and Lara had been in his cabin – and now he was turning toward the open ocean.

The deck was treacherous, and they almost fell twice, but they managed to reach the bridge without injury. Lara tried to open the door, but it was locked. There was a window next to the door, and they could see Andrew through it. The lights were on inside, and he stood before the ship's controls, steering the vessel. His face was a mask of grim determination, and his eyes blazed with something akin to madness.

Lara pounded on the window with the flat of her hand.

"Dad! Let us in!"

There was no way Andrew couldn't have heard her, even over the sounds of the storm and the ship's engine. But he didn't turn to look at her.

She pounded some more and shouted louder this time.

"Goddamn it, Dad! What the *fuck* are you doing?"

Still no reaction from Andrew. He continued looking straight ahead as he steered the *Wayfarer* away from the dock.

Lara made a fist and frantically slammed it against the glass over and over.

"*Dad!*"

* * * * *

Andrew heard his daughter, of course. He wasn't deaf. But right then, he didn't have time to deal with her – or Joel. The only reason he'd allowed that fucker to accompany them was because he needed the camera, and having another pair of hands along to help fight the pliosaurs had been useful. But now that he had the camera, he was confident he could get the video off of it despite the water damage it had sustained. And if he couldn't, he would hire someone who could. His one regret was not being able to find a way to steal the pliosaur's corpse and sneak it on board, but he was content with what he had. It would be enough. And he believed the video footage of the mega-pliosaurs that Owen had captured would be what convinced the world that the entire species was a threat which needed to be eliminated. The video of the smaller pliosaurs killing people had ignited the fire, but when the public saw the mega-pliosaurs destroying the catamaran, like monsters from ancient myth brought to life, their fear would intensify to the point of hysteria, and not even the most dedicated animal rights activists would be able to sway them into viewing them as anything but … what had Tomas called them? *Devils.* After that, it would be open season on the bastards, and once humans were aware of them, they wouldn't stand a chance. Humans were geniuses when it came to killing. They'd wiped out entire species many times before, and with luck, they would do so again, and the pliosaurs would become what they should've been all along – ancient history.

He didn't believe in an afterlife, so he didn't think his wife Barbara was looking down on him from the lofty vantage point of some cosmic paradise. But even so, if there was the slightest chance that some part of her being still existed somewhere, he hoped she would rest easier now.

* * * * *

One-Eye had lost a significant amount of blood, but he kept on swimming, even though all he wanted to do was close his remaining eye, rise to the surface, and float there while he slept. But with a mass of hungry nestlings invading the canals, to sleep now would be to die.

He still maintained his grip on the dead soft-skin, one leg in his mouth, the rest of the body folded back against his head and neck, held there by the current. The soft-skin flopped against his neck wounds now and again, sending fiery bolts of pain shooting through his body, but the pain was welcome. It helped him to stay awake, spurred him to continue onward in his search for the females. He had no sense of how long he'd been wandering the canals looking for them. His kind reckoned time by light sky and dark sky, by the rhythms of their body, by the moon and the tides. But he felt as tired as if he'd made the sojourn to the Beginning Place all over again, although he did not think he had swum that far.

He knew Whiteback's and Nub's scents as intimately as he knew his brother's and his own, and since the females were gravid with eggs and ready to nest soon, their scents were stronger than normal. Finding them should have been a simple matter, and yet so far he hadn't –

And then he found it: a subtle hint of Whiteback's scent. He oriented on it at once and began tracing it. Her scent trail grew stronger with every foot he swam, and then he could smell Nub's scent, too. His kind knew nothing of hope, but he felt something akin to a primitive version of that emotion now, and tired and weak as he was, he swam faster.

He had no conception of where he was in relation to Elysium. The land the canals wound through meant no more to him than a place where the soft-skins walked. But he finally found Whiteback and Nub in a stretch of canal on the West Shore, not far from where they'd killed Echo Amato. They were heading back to the ocean, ready to circle the island and locate a suitable strand of beach where they could deposit their eggs.

When One-Eye caught up to them, he lowered his head, arched his back, and allowed his flippers to hang limply at his sides. This was the posture of a submissive male, and though he once would've fought to the death to establish dominance over another pliosaur, even them, he was far too weak to do so now.

The females turned toward him, intrigued by the scent of his offering and the smell of his blood. What had One-Eye brought them and what had happened to him?

They recognized his posture at once, and they held their flippers straight out from their sides, raised their heads, and showed their teeth in displays of dominance. Then they came forward to examine the offering he had brought. They smelled it, bumped it with their snouts, and when they deemed it acceptable, they each took hold of a different part of it. Whiteback bit down on the soft-skin's head, and Nub took its free leg in her mouth.

One-Eye released his hold on the soft-skin and retreated several yards to show he had no interest in claiming any of the meat for himself. The females tore into their unexpected gift, and even though their bellies were full from the feasting they'd done since reaching the island, they tore apart the soft-skin's body and swallowed the pieces with enthusiasm. There was always room in a pliosaur's stomach for a little more.

When they finished, all that was left of Tammy Chu was a red cloud of slowly dissipating blood.

The females looked at One-Eye then and assessed his physical state. He had brought them meat and they had found it pleasing, but he was wounded, and while still a ways from death, he was too weak to fight. If they allowed him to accompany them, they would be forced to protect him. On any other day, they might have been willing to do so. But today, egg-laying had come, and neither of them could afford to take time nursemaiding One-Eye, not in his current condition.

Whiteback and Nub moved in unspoken agreement. They shot toward One-Eye, and Whiteback fastened her teeth around his neck – right where Shayne had shot him – and Nub bit into the soft flesh of his underbelly. Then they gave two sharp pulls in opposite directions, and One-Eye's head tore free from his body, releasing more blood to cloud the water. The females dropped the two pieces of his body, and they sank to the canal bottom, leaving a pair of blood trails behind them. Neither female bothered with eating him. They were full to bursting already, and their bodies demanded they find a nesting place *now*.

They turned and continued swimming toward the ocean, the memory of One-Eye fading from their simple minds as they went.

CHAPTER TWENTY- SIX

The bridge's windows were made with reinforced glass to withstand the strongest storms. Even so, Andrew thought Lara might break through if she continued striking the window like this. He didn't want to leave her out in the rain, although he had no problem doing that to Joel. But he couldn't let her onto the bridge, not yet. He couldn't risk her or Joel wresting control of the *Wayfarer* from him. Not until they were far enough out to sea that it would be too late to turn back, and they would agree the best course of action would be to continue on to the mainland. Once they were away from the island and the horrible experiences they'd had there, maybe he could talk some reason into them, make them see why the pliosaurs needed to be killed, every last one of them. He thought he could convince Lara. After all, a mega-pliosaur had killed her mother. They'd both witnessed it, although Lara had been so little, she had only fragmentary memories at best. She might not want revenge against the foul creatures as much as he did, but given how many people she'd see the *Las Dagas* Monsters kill today, he thought she'd come around sooner rather than later. As for Joel … Andrew had never found it easy to predict how the man would act in a given situation. Maybe he'd see things Andrew's way, maybe he wouldn't. He might well try to destroy the evidence Andrew had gathered in a misguided attempt to protect the pliosaurs. But he wouldn't let that happen. Once they were far enough away from the island and the storm let up, he would find a way to deal with Joel. He didn't have any guns aboard, but he had spearfishing equipment. A shot through the heart, the body tossed over the railing, and voila! Problem solved.

But for now, Lara and Joel were just going to have to seek shelter somewhere else on the ship or keep standing on deck getting rained on. It made no difference to him.

* * * * *

Lara continued pounding on the window until Joel pulled her back.

"Come on, let's get out of the rain."

For a moment, it looked like she might argue, but then she nodded and led him aft again. The storm hadn't let up one iota. If anything, it had gotten worse. Thunder and lightning came more often, louder and brighter, and the winds were practically at gale force. Frigid rain hit their bodies like sharp pellets of ice, and the ship rocked side to side, up and down, forward and back as Andrew made for open water. Joel and Lara held tight to the railing as they went, but it was slow, dangerous going. Eventually, they reached the main cabin and went in. Joel quickly shut the door behind them, and even though the storm continued to rage outside and they were soaked to the bone, it felt fantastic to be inside. It was quieter in here, too, at least a little.

"Stay here for a s-second," Lara said, barely able to get the words past chattering teeth. She went through a door that led to another room, and when she came back, she was carrying a pair of gray woolen blankets. She gave one to Joel and kept one for herself. They wrapped the blankets around themselves, and while Joel was still cold and wet, he was instantly warmer than he had been a moment earlier.

A small table with U-shaped bench seating was attached to the wall, and the cabin had a compact stove, a refrigerator, and a microwave on a counter beneath some cupboards. The ship was tossing so much that they sat at the table and held onto the edge to brace themselves.

"Not to put too fine a point on it," Joel said, "but I think your dad's gone bat-shit crazy. Where the hell is he headed? And why would he risk going out in these conditions?"

"I honestly don't know." She sounded distraught. "This isn't like him at all. He's usually so calm, so rational …" She frowned, thinking. "He took Mom's death hard, and he's had to deal with the ridicule of the scientific community ever since. I'd hoped that learning pliosaurs still exist and actually seeing them would be healing for him. But it had to have brought back some awful memories for him. I know it did for me. And seeing so many people killed, just like Mom was …"

Joel understood. That sort of psychological pressure could get to anyone.

"So he's … what? Trying to get away from the pliosaurs and the emotions they stir in him?"

"Maybe. Or maybe he doesn't want to see me die the way Mom did."

Both of these theories seemed plausible to Joel. After everything that had happened, Andrew had developed an irresistible compulsion to leave *Las Dagas,* and he'd locked them out of the bridge so they couldn't stop him from going out into the storm.

All of this might be true, but Joel didn't think it was the *entire* truth. But he didn't see what either of them could do about it now. Yeah, they could possibly find some kind of tool – a hammer or maybe a fire ax – and use it to break into the bridge. But what would they do then? Attack Andrew and try to restrain him? Lara could pilot the vessel, so they'd have that covered. But what if something went wrong when they rushed Andrew? He might accidentally yank the steering wheel the wrong way, and in these conditions, they could end up capsizing. And with all the pliosaurs in the area …

A terrible thought occurred to him then. An awful, horrifying thought. Lara and he had been so focused on reaching the *Wayfarer* and calling Ysmin on the satellite phone, and so distracted by Andrew's behavior that they'd forgotten one extremely important detail.

"The mega-pliosaurs," he said. "We watched them sink a catamaran. And if they could do that …"

Lara paled.

"They could do the same to us."

* * * * *

Full night had fallen, and with the storm clouds still hanging over the island, it was darker than the inside of Satan's ass. Andrew had turned on the *Wayfarer's* running lights as they'd left the dock, but they did little to cut through the darkness. And of course with all this rain, visibility was for shit. None of that really mattered, though. He was perfectly capable of sailing by instruments alone, had done so many times over the years. All he wanted to do was get past this storm, and he didn't much care what direction they were heading in.

Now that they'd been out in this insane weather for a while, his white-hot determination to get the hell off *Las Dagas* immediately and carry proof of the pliosaurs' existence to the world was starting to cool. He felt like a man who was waking from a dream, or maybe more like someone who'd been drunk out of his mind and was starting to sober up. Heading back to civilization – such as it was – was one thing. But sailing in these conditions? And with his daughter aboard? What the hell had he been thinking, risking her life like this? Joel's life, too. He might despise the man, but that didn't mean he wanted to see him dead. Or did he? Hadn't he been thinking about shooting him with a spear gun? He guessed he had, but the thought seemed so alien now.

He still thought the pliosaurs were a threat to humanity, still believed they should be exterminated. But he was starting to have some doubts in this area, too. He'd kept telling everyone the pliosaurs were only animals, kept pretending that he didn't want anyone to hurt them, but he'd only done those things to disguise his true feelings. But what if the pliosaurs weren't devils after all? Ultimately, they weren't all that different from humans. They did what they had to in order to survive.

So he was having second thoughts. What if Ahab had changed his mind about getting vengeance on the white whale that had taken his leg? What if he'd turned the *Pequod* around and headed back to Nantucket? A lot of lives would've been saved, including his own. Could Andrew turn around at this point and go back to *Las Dagas*? Or would it be safer to keep plowing through the storm toward the mainland? He supposed he could get on the radio, see if he could reach another ship in the general vicinity, maybe find out if they had any idea what direction the storm was going. After that, he'd choose whichever course of action appeared to be the safest.

He picked up the mike and held it to his mouth. But before he could speak, lightning flashed outside the *Wayfarer*, illuminating a nightmarish scene. Directly in front of the ship. Two mega-pliosaurs were fighting. The gigantic creatures slammed their huge bodies together, snapping and biting, tearing out mouthfuls of flesh and spitting them out. They churned the already turbulent seawater to white froth as they battled. Lightning came again and again, creating an eerie strobe light effect as the *Wayfarer* sailed closer to the two monsters. Both were bleeding from numerous wounds, but their injuries only appeared to goad them into fighting more fiercely.

Andrew was momentarily mesmerized by the primal savagery on display before him, but he forced himself to focus. There was still time to avoid the mega-pliosaurs. All he had to do was turn the ship hard to starboard and they'd pass by the monsters. The behemoths were so wrapped up in trying to kill one another that they probably wouldn't notice the *Wayfarer* going by.

He dropped the mike and put both hands on the steering controls, but he hesitated.

These things looked *exactly* like the one that had killed his wife. He supposed it was even possible that one of them *was* the same beast. But even if neither of them was the exact monster that had killed his Barbara, they were close enough.

"Fuck you," he snarled, and instead of turning the ship, he pushed the throttle all the way forward to the ship's maximum speed.

* * * * *

The Matriarch ripped a chunk of neck flesh from the female that had killed the Sire, and she spit the bloody hunk of meat into the water and attacked again. The mega-pliosaurs fought on the surface because they needed to breathe to engage in this kind of physical activity. Underwater skirmishes were brief by necessity, but true battles, ones where the opponents fought with no quarter given or asked, tearing each other apart one bite at a time – those were fought on the surface.

The other female swung her head toward the Matriarch and struck her mouth. The female took some damage from the Matriarch's teeth, but she managed to knock a number of them out, so it was a decent trade-off. A pliosaur's teeth were its first, best weapon, and when they were gone, the entire animal soon followed.

The Matriarch hissed in fury, and she was about to go for the other female's eyes when light caught her attention. Not lightning. She knew what that was. This was different. It did not flash bright and then die way. This light was constant. And accompanying it was a low thrumming sound that she recognized as belonging to one of the hard-shelled things that the soft-skins sometimes traveled in, like the things she and the Sire had destroyed earlier. This hard-shell came directly at them, and before either female could react, the *Wayfarer* crashed into them both.

* * * * *

There was a deafening noise, the sound of some great impact, and the *Wayfarer* lurched violently to port. Joel and Lara slammed against the wall, and then fell off the bench to land sprawled on the floor. The ship listed beneath them, and they helped each other to stand and made their way to the door across the tilted floor. Their blankets had fallen off them during the collision – it *had* to have been a collision, couldn't have been anything else – and when they stepped back out onto the deck, they were once more struck with bitterly cold rain. They needed to use the rail more than ever now, for the *Wayfarer*'s bow was tilted forward, and the angle was increasing.

"We're going down!" Joel said.

"We have to get Dad!"

Lara didn't wait for him to respond. She steadied herself with the railing as she made her way toward the bridge.

"Fuck!" Joel shouted, and then followed.

But before they could reach Andrew, a huge dark shape rose up before the ship. Lightning flashed, illuminating the Matriarch. Half of her head was a bloody, ragged ruin, but for the moment, she still lived. The same couldn't be said of her opponent, who was sinking toward the ocean floor, a dark cloud of blood trailing from the gaping wound in her half-severed neck.

The Matriarch flung herself onto the front half of the *Wayfarer*, obliterating the bridge and crushing Andrew to a paste of blood, meat, and shattered bone. The ship shuddered, and Joel grabbed hold of Lara with one hand while holding tight to the railing with the other. Lara screamed as the Matriarch breathed her last.

Seeing the mega-pliosaur crash onto the ship momentarily drove all thought from Joel's mind. But when the bow tilted even further downward, he knew they had run out of time. He forced himself to forget what had happened – at least for now – and focus on trying to stay alive.

"We have to get off the ship! We need life jackets or life preservers!"

Lara no longer screamed, but she was staring at the corpse of the mega-pliosaur. Joel thought she hadn't heard him, but she turned away from the monster that had killed her father – the same breed of creature that had killed her mother – and faced him.

"That's a *terrible* idea. If we jumped into the water as rough as it is right now, we'd drown in minutes, even with flotation devices. I have a better idea. Come on!"

She gripped the railing and started pulling herself upward toward the aft of the ship. Joel did the same. He didn't know what her idea was, but he hoped it was a hell of a good one.

CHAPTER TWENTY- SEVEN

Two months later, six helicopters bearing the Lexana logo flew over placid blue water toward *Las Dagas*. The sky was clear, the sun bright, wind minimal. Perfect flying weather.

The storm that had ravaged the island sixty-three days earlier had caused a fair amount of damage to Elysium's buildings, but by and large, the resort remained intact. Elysium was, however, deserted. Aside from a handful of researchers who Lexana had set up on the island, every human who had been on *Las Dagas* the morning after the storm passed – resort guests and employees alike – had left as soon as they could. Some because they refused to remain in a place where actual monsters had killed a lot of people, and others because Lexana had quietly paid them to relocate. What precisely the corporation intended to do with *Las Dagas* wasn't clear, and Joel didn't think he wanted to know.

He was a passenger in one of the helicopters, along with Lara, who sat close beside him, holding his hand. They were strapped into their seats, wore headsets, and both had high-powered binoculars resting on both their laps. They had become celebrities of a sort after that awful night, and Joel sometimes wondered what Shayne would've thought of that if he were still alive. They'd become the public faces of the discovery that a species of prehistoric creature still existed in modern times. They'd given hundreds of interviews, landed a book deal, and soon they would start filming a documentary on their experiences with the pliosaurs. The species even had a proper scientific name now: *Pliosauroidea Rivera*. The scientific community had agreed to name the species after Andrew, as both a tribute and apology to the man. Joel thought Andrew would've been both pleased and honored.

Lexana had been good to them. After all, they were what corporate types called "brand ambassadors," even if they weren't technically employed by Lexana. But the corporation had helped them in others ways, like inviting them to ride along today.

This was the first time they'd been back to the island since the night Andrew died and the *Wayfarer* sank. They'd escaped going down with the ship themselves thanks to the inflatable motorized raft that Andrew and Lara had used for short trips away from the *Wayfarer* to collect samples of sea life for their research. Piloting the thing through the storm-stirred waters had been dicey as hell, and they'd almost capsized a couple times, but Lara knew what she was doing, and eventually, they'd reached a place where the storm wasn't as strong, and the going was easier after that. Best of all, they hadn't encountered a single damn pliosaur, regular or super-size.

After the female pliosaurs had made nests on the beaches and deposited their eggs within, they'd returned to the sea, and soon after, all of the pliosaur pods departed, scattering to whatever parts of the world's oceans they usually called home. Lexana moved in soon afterward. A number of dead specimens had been recovered, although none were entirely intact. And while it had taken some work, Lexana even managed to raise the bodies of a couple mega-pliosaurs. Joel and Lara didn't know if the monster that had sunk the *Wayfarer* was one of them, and they never intended to find out.

The pilot's voice came over their headsets then.

"*This is it,*" she said. "*Some of the eggs started hatching yesterday, but it looks like the rest of them decided to pick today as their birthday.*"

The helicopters hovered over one of the island's beaches. They were forbidden to land or come too close to the hatchlings. No one knew exactly how rare this species was, but it wasn't as if pliosaur nests were common on the world's beaches, so until more was understood about the animals, Lexana intended to maintain a strict policy of non-contact. This meant regular air and sea patrols to prevent the curious and the greedy from trying to sneak onto the island.

Joel and Lara unfastened their seat straps, took hold of their binoculars, and went to a window. The pilot angled the helicopter to give them a better view, and they raised the binoculars to their eyes and gazed down at the beach.

Hundreds of baby pliosaurs were racing across the sand toward the ocean, tiny flippers working like mad. No one had known for sure what the gestation period for pliosaur eggs would be. Lara had told him that sea turtle eggs hatched in two months, and alligator eggs had an incubation period of sixty-five days. So around two months had seemed like a safe bet, and obviously it had been.

"They're so tiny, they're almost cute," Joel said.

As they watched, a sea gull flew over the beach and dipped down toward several of the babies. For a moment, Joel thought the gull was going to have itself a nice snack, but when the bird was almost upon them, four of the baby pliosaurs leaped upward and sank small but needle-sharp teeth into the gull. They brought the bird to the ground, and as it flapped its wings futilely, a dozen more baby pliosaurs rushed toward it and all began feeding. Within seconds, the sand was stained red with the gull's blood, and the babies were covered in crimson.

Lara lowered her binoculars and looked at Joel. He shrugged.

"I said *almost*."

AUTHOR BIO

Tim Waggoner has published close to forty novels and three collections of short stories. He writes original dark fantasy and horror, as well as media tie-ins, and his articles on writing have appeared in numerous publications. He's won the Bram Stoker Award, been a finalist for the Shirley Jackson Award and the Scribe Award, his fiction has received numerous Honorable Mentions in volumes of *Best Horror of the Year*, and he's twice had stories selected for inclusion in volumes of *Year's Best Hardcore Horror*. He's also a full-time tenured professor who teaches creative writing and composition at Sinclair College in Dayton, Ohio.

CHECK OUT OTHER GREAT DEEP SEA THRILLERS

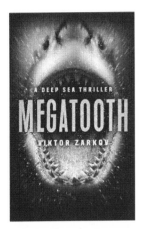

MEGATOOTH
by Viktor Zarkov

When the death rate of sperm whales rises dramatically, a well-respected environmental activist puts together a ragtag team to hit the high seas to investigate the matter. They suspect that the deaths are due to poachers and they are all driven by a need for justice.

Elsewhere, an experimental government vessel is enhancing deep sea mining equipment. They see one of these dead whales up close and personal...and are fairly certain that it wasn't poachers that killed it.

Both of these teams are about to discover that poachers are the least of their worries. There is something hunting the whales...

Something big
Something prehistoric.
Something terrifying.
MEGATOOTH!

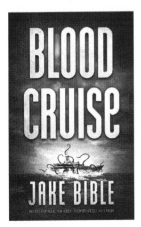

BLOOD CRUISE
by Jake Bible

Ben Clow's plans are set. Drop off kids, pick up girlfriend, head to the marina, and hop on best friend's cruiser for a weekend of fun at sea. But Ben's happy plans are about to be changed by a tentacled horror that lurks beneath the waves.

International crime lords! Deep cover black ops agents! A ravenous, bloodsucking monster! A storm of evil and danger conspire to turn Ben Clow's vacation from a fun ocean getaway into a nightmare of a Blood Cruise!

CHECK OUT OTHER GREAT DEEP SEA THRILLERS

SEA RAPTOR
by John J. Rust

From terrorist hunter to monster hunter! Jack Rastun was a decorated U.S. Army Ranger, until an unfortunate incident forced him out of the service. He is soon hired by the Foundation for Undocumented Biological Investigation and given a new mission, to search for cryptids, creatures whose existence has not been proven by mainstream science. Teaming up with the daring and beautiful wildlife photographer Karen Thatcher, they must stop a sea monster's deadly rampage along the Jersey Shore. But that's not the only danger Rastun faces. A group of murderous animal smugglers also want the creature. Rastun must utilize every skill learned from years of fighting, otherwise, his first mission for the FUBI might very well be his last.

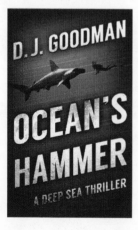

OCEAN'S HAMMER
by D.J. Goodman

Something strange is happening in the Sea of Cortez. Whales are beaching for no apparent reason and the local hammerhead shark population, previously believed to be fished to extinction, has suddenly reappeared. Marine biologists Maria Quintero and Kevin Hoyt have come to investigate with a television producer in tow, hoping to get footage that will land them a reality TV show. The plan is to have a stand-off against a notorious illegal shark-fishing captain and then go home.

Things are not going according to plan.

There is something new in the waters of the Sea of Cortez. Something smart. Something huge. Something that has its own plans for Quintero and Hoyt.

CHECK OUT OTHER GREAT DEEP SEA THRILLERS

PREHISTORIC BEASTS AND WHERE TO FIGHT THEM
by Hugo Navikov

IN THE DEPTHS, SOMETHING WAITS ...

Acclaimed film director Jake Bentneus pilots a custom submersible to the bottom of Challenger Deep in the Pacific, the deepest point of any ocean of Earth. But something lurks at the hot hydrothermal vents, a creature—a dinosaur—too big to exist.

Gigadon.

It not only exists, but it follows him, hungrily, back to the surface. Later, a barely living Bentneus offers a $1 billion prize to anyone who can find and kill the monster. His best bet is renowned ichthyopaleontologist Sean Muir, who had predicted adapted dinosaurs lived at the bottom of the ocean.

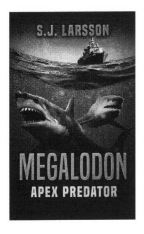

MEGALODON: APEX PREDATOR
by S.J. Larsson

English adventurer Sir Jeffery Mallory charters a ship for a top secret expedition to Antarctica. What starts out as a search and capture mission soon turns into a terrifying fight for survival as the crew come face to face with the fiercest ocean predator to have ever existed- Carcharodon Megalodon. Alone and with no hope of rescue the crew will need all their resources if they are to survive not only a 60 foot shark but also the harsh Antarctic conditions. Megalodon: Apex Predator is a deep-sea adventure filled with action, twists and savage prehistoric sharks.

85601666R00109

Made in the USA
Columbia, SC
02 January 2018